Donated to the El Camino College Library

by

SOUTH BAY
QUILTERS
GUILD

A
STITCH
IN
TIME

Also by Ann Rinaldi:

In My Father's House
Wolf by the Ears

The Quilt Trilogy

A STITCH IN TIME

Ann Rinaldi

SCHOLASTIC HARDCOVER

Scholastic Inc.
New York

Library of Congress Cataloging-in-Publication Data

Rinaldi, Ann.
    A stitch in time / Ann Rinaldi.

        p.   cm.—(Quilt trilogy ; #1)
    Summary: Shortly after the War of Independence, Hannah sees her family being torn apart by old secrets and new developments, as her sister resolves to marry a sea captain and other siblings prepare to help start a new town in the Northwestern Territory.

ISBN 0-590-46055-2

    [1. Family life—Fiction. 2. Quilting—Fiction. 3. Frontier and pioneer life—Fiction.]   I. Title.   II. Series: Rinaldi, Ann. Quilt trilogy ; #1. PZ7.R459St   1994   [Fic]—dc20   93-8964
                                                                                                  CIP
                                                                                                  AC

12   11   10   9   8   7   6   5   4   3   2   6   7   8   9/9

Printed in the U.S.A.   37

First printing, April 1994

*In memory of my
Aunt Teresa
1903–1993,
who first encouraged
me to be a writer, and
who, like Hannah, was
there for everyone in
the family*

Acknowledgments

I am, once again, indebted to the historians, amateur and professional, who wrote the wonderful books I used for my research. Without their efforts, their endless chronicles of facts, I would not have been able to write this book. For it was from the books mentioned in the accompanying bibliography that I, a lay person and student of American history, learned the trade routes of Salem's vessels, the architecture of the ships, as well as the lives of the seamen and the merchants of Salem. My gratitude is heartfelt to these writers. Any mistakes I made, however, are mine, and not any fault of theirs.

Thanks go to John Fraylor, park historian at the Salem Maritime National Historical Site, Salem, Massachusetts, for his patience in answering so many questions.

I am indebted, also, to the staff at the Essex Institute in Salem, for advising me about reading material. And to the staffs at the Peabody Museum, and the National Park Service Visitor Center for their assistance.

Thanks, once again, must go to my son, Ronald P. Rinaldi II, for use of his marvelous library on American and military history. The years we spent as a family, reenacting the battles and encampments of the American Revolution, with Ron's encouragement, are priceless for their memories alone, but those times also served as a catalyst for my own interest in history. Thanks also goes to my husband for his patience and support; to my daughter, Marcella, for her respect for my "writer's space"; to my publisher, Scholastic; and my editor, Regina Griffin, for their faith in me.

A
STITCH
IN
TIME

The Chelmsford Family

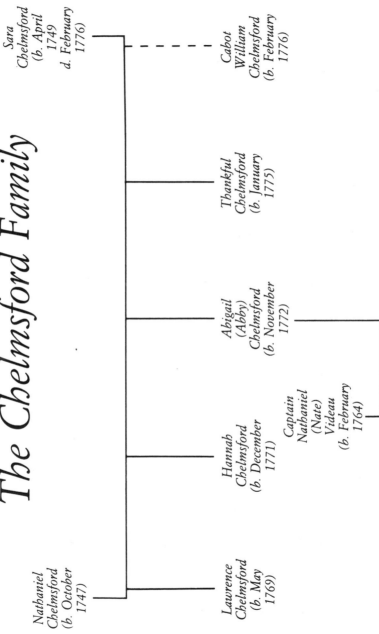

Nathaniel Chelmsford (b. October 1747)

Sara Chelmsford (b. April 1749 d. February 1776)

Lawrence Chelmsford (b. May 1769)

Hannah Chelmsford (b. December 1771)

Captain Nathaniel (Nate) Videau (b. February 1764)

Abigail (Abby) Chelmsford (b. November 1772)

Thankful Chelmsford (b. January 1775)

Cabot William Chelmsford (b. February 1776)

Prologue

The boy tied the woolen scarf tighter around his neck. The morning mist was cold, rolling in off the water. He peered anxiously through it, eager to sight the ship through the thickness.

Twelve-year-old Cabot William Chelmsford knew how quickly the curtain of fog could part to reveal the wondrous sights around him that he so loved. Salem's wharves were his second home.

Its ships' masters allowed him to carry their personal baggage off and on their vessels. He listened to their conversations, learned of their cargoes and destinations, memorized the colors of the pennants flown by every merchant house in town.

Now he was waiting to sight a ship owned by Elias Hasket Derby, the richest merchant in Salem. The *Cheerful Sally* should be rounding Naugus Head within the half hour on its return voyage from Bordeaux after sixteen months at sea.

Derby gave a gold coin to the first boy to sight his returning ships. And Cabot was determined to have the gold coin this day.

"Did y'all sight her yet, mate?"

The voice, tinged with a molasses drawl, loomed overhead, disembodied, from the quarterdeck of the *Swamp Fox*. Then the form of Captain Nate Videau came through the fog. He stood there bold as brass, sipping his morning coffee in his nankeen trousers and woolen jacket. The kind of man Cabot wanted to be.

"Not yet, sir."

Videau consulted a gold pocketwatch. "She'll be here within twenty minutes. Mind what ah say, boy."

Videau was up from Charleston, South Carolina, with a load of rice and indigo from his father's plantation. Yesterday Cabot had sat in Videau's cabin while the man had calculated the arrival time of the *Cheerful Sally*. Derby had word of the *Sally*'s departure time from one of his captains who'd arrived yesterday, and Videau had made the same voyage himself.

"Tomorrow morning," Videau had said. "Near six bells."

The man was audacious and courageous. Cabot had complete faith in him. All his friends would be looking to sight the *Sally* in the afternoon.

"Did Richard Lander give you an arrival time?" Videau asked now.

"No, sir. He's been too busy working on the *Black Prince*."

Videau nodded. "He's having her hull coppered

today. She'll be ready to sail soon. Where to, nobody knows. It's the best kept secret in the Commonwealth."

"Lots of people think he's outfitting the *Prince* for the slave trade," Cabot said.

"What would Nathaniel Chelmsford think about that?" Videau asked.

The *Black Prince* had been the ship dearest to Cabot's father's heart, he knew. His best brigantine, turned into a privateer during the Revolution. It had been burned in the Penobscot Expedition in '79 and had sat in dry dock until this year, when Lander began to restore it.

"My father says slavers are morally depraved," Cabot said.

Videau burst into laughter. "No wonder your daddy hates me. My father, brother-in-law, and ah, enjoy the fruits of the business." Then he scowled. "But New Englanders enjoy the fruits of the business, too. There are many different kinds of moral depravity, boy."

"Yes, sir." Cabot had no idea what kind of moral depravity Videau alluded to, but where his father was concerned, he'd believe just about any kind Videau came up with.

Of course, the man mentioned Abby, Cabot's fifteen-year-old sister. "Do y'all think it isn't morally depraved for your daddy to keep Abby locked in her room for three days just because ah've dropped anchor in port?"

Cabot nodded in agreement. He knew Videau was seething over the matter. Not that Cabot blamed him one bit.

"It was the same with my last two visits," Videau recounted.

Cabot nodded. Videau and Abby were in love and had a right to be together. *Somebody* in his family had a right to be happy. And he had done his best to help them, delivering notes and messages, acting as a go-between. He wished he could do more.

"Do you think Lander's going to use the *Prince* for the slave trade?" he asked. Videau was gazing moodily off into the mists and Cabot wanted to keep the conversation going.

"No. It's too financially risky and the man's determined to become richer than Derby so he can court your sister Hannah. Y'all know he's sweet on her. Or so Abby suspects."

"Hannah won't hear of it. She said if I mention Lander's name to her she'll box my ears, good."

Videau laughed. "That's got nothing to do with her being smitten with him, boy."

"It doesn't?" He had thought Hannah was still languishing over Louis Gaudineer, her Pennsylvania militiaman, who had gone west and whom their father had forbidden her to marry.

"Some people," Videau explained, "just go about being in love like mules going up a hill backward."

Cabot smiled to himself. If Hannah did love Lander he could help her. The way he'd helped Abby. As with Videau, this would endear him to Lander. Both men had already taught him a lot about the sea. And could teach much more. "Lander's teaching me to use the octant," he told Videau. "And I'm learning to furl a sail and stand a trick at the wheel."

"Good," Videau said. "A man should always be prepared to follow his course when the opportunity presents itself."

Cabot's heart skipped a beat. Videau was *planning* something! Something to do with Abigail! He could feel it in his bones. But how to find out?

"What's in your cargo?" he asked. You could find out a lot about a ship master's plans by what was in his hold.

"Ah've got 101,000 feet of plank and joist. Intend to load on 78,000 staves and 41,000 feet of ranging timber. As well as spermaceti candles. Then ah'll be picking up molasses, sugar, and coffee for my return trip."

"That means the West Indies," Cabot said.

"That's right, boy."

"When do you clear?"

"Next week. Night of your daddy's party."

Night of the party! The man had cheek! *Were he and Abby planning something the night of the party?* "Abby will be sad to see you go."

Videau smiled, fished inside his coat pocket, and

withdrew a letter. "Don't intend to leave her sad. Don't intend to leave her at all, 's'matter of fact. Would y'all deliver this note to her today?"

Cabot thought he would die. "Be happy to, sir."

Videau brushed the note with his lips and dropped it down. Cabot caught it.

"Next week. The night of the party," Videau drawled, "ah intend to climb up to the widow's walk of your house and fetch Abby. And we'll clear Salem Harbor that night. But first we marry, to make everything real proper like."

"Marry?" Cabot could barely get the word past his lips.

"Right on this quarterdeck. Ah've got it all planned. Got that nice Reverend Cutler from Ipswich. Your sister Hannah helped with that, bless her."

Cabot's head was spinning. *Marry. Run away. Right under his father's nose.* The audacity of the plan thrilled him. He would miss Abby, his freckle-faced, tawny-haired, laughing sister, of course. There would only be Hannah then, who, though only a year older than Abby, took the responsibility of a mother in the house and never laughed enough. And Thankful, who was thirteen and the plague of his life. Then something else came to him. Videau would be his brother-in-law.

"Would you let me sign on with you someday, Captain Nate?"

"In a few years. If you finish your schooling first and promise not to run away to sea."

"You ran away to fight with Francis Marion, the Swamp Fox."

"Ah didn't run away. My sister was giving him aid. My father made me wait until ah was sixteen. Now y'all promise, or y'all will hear from me."

Cabot promised. And the man who had fought with the Swamp Fox pointed then. "Ahoy, boy. Look there."

Cabot looked. The sun had broken through the mists. And there was the *Cheerful Sally*, rounding Naugus Head, sails billowing like angels' wings. Oh, she was so beautiful, gliding along so majestically. Cabot felt his blood tingle. "The *Cheerful Sally*," he yelled. "She's here!"

People came running through the fog from all directions. "Thank you, Captain Videau," he said.

"Y'all be sure and tell Derby that her signal flags indicate all is well on board." The Southern voice cut through the fog as Cabot ran toward the counting house. "And any time y'all want to know anything about the sea, y'all come to me."

Ten minutes later, with his gold coin clutched in his fist, Cabot made his way along the shoreline to where the *Black Prince* lay on her side, like a dying whale. He wanted to see Richard Lander with fresh eyes now that he knew the man was setting about to make his fortune to court Hannah. Perhaps he could help him somehow.

Lander was under an old Revolutionary War marque, pouring over drawings on a desk. Near the *Prince* three men were standing around a tripod on which was a large pot of boiling liquid. The bottom of the *Prince* had been scrubbed clean of encrusted growths and was already coated with sulphur, resin, and tallow to make it watertight. Now it would be coppered.

Cabot watched the carpenters and caulkers and painters climbing all over the ship. Then he walked through the piles of wood chips, into the marque, the stench of sulphur and resin in his nose.

"Good morning, Captain Lander."

Lander nodded. "What are you about so early?"

"I was the first to sight the *Cheerful Sally*. I got the gold coin."

"What kind of condition is she in?"

"Don't know. But Captain Videau said her signal flags indicate all's well on board. He figured the arrival time for me."

"Smart man." Lander smiled. "How many notes have you delivered to Abigail for him?"

"How do you know that?"

"My sister works in your house, remember?"

"Your sister doesn't have a loose tongue. Everybody's been asking her where you're taking the *Prince*. She won't tell."

"She doesn't know. You think I'd burden a fifteen-year-old girl with that knowledge?"

"It must be to the other side of the world," Cabot said.

Lander laughed quietly. "I'm going to give

Derby a run for his money. And it's going to be lucrative."

Cabot said nothing. He had been taking Lander's measure. The man had a reputation for fairness, hard work, and hard play. He was as solemn as the wealthiest codfish aristocrat in town, not fun-loving like Videau. Yet Cabot knew Lander enjoyed his ale at Goodhue's Tavern, where merchants conducted their business, that Lander attended cockfights, and that when he stood on the sideline at turtle frolics or pig roasts, the girls all swooned over his good looks.

He had no one girl on his arm, but many. Ofttimes, Cabot had seen him with disreputable women from the wharves. He was careful never to mention that to Hannah.

Cabot studied him with fresh eyes, sizing him up as a husband for Hannah. He was ruddy of complexion, blue of eye, and wiry of build. Not as tall as Videau, but his jaw was set and strong and when he looked at you, you paid mind.

Yes, Cabot decided, I will help bring matters along between him and Hannah.

But there was one matter to clear up, first. There was in Lander, something like the eye of a storm. You feared it, yet were drawn to it at the same time. Cabot had always known it had to do with the war. And his own father. He'd grown up knowing there was bad blood between the two families. Time, he decided, to find out why.

"Captain Lander, what happened between our families during the war?" he asked.

Lander looked up sharply, then back down at his drawings. "Why bring that up, boy? There's no profit in the telling."

"I've always wanted to ask and at home they shush me. There are so many secrets in our house, I can't abide it."

Lander smiled. "It's not a happy house. And I suppose you're old enough to know. Back in '74, the Continental Congress called for an end of export trade with Britain, Ireland, and the British West Indies as of September of '75. In November of '75 one of your father's brigs was caught carrying dry fish for Jamaica."

Cabot waited.

"When your father learned that a legislative committee was about to investigate the matter he came to my father, who often captained for him. He asked my father to take the blame for going against regulations. He promised to reimburse him well and always to take care of our family, financially. Well, my father agreed. He needed the money."

"New England merchants have always smuggled," Cabot said.

"True," Lander allowed, "a certain amount of judicious smuggling is tradition. But we were already at war here in New England. My father was disgraced. He killed himself."

Cabot's ears buzzed. His mouth went dry. He couldn't speak.

"That's why your father took me into his counting house and my mother gets a monthly stipend from him," Lander said. "She never spent it. That's how I got the money to restore the *Prince*."

"My father's not a very nice man, is he?" Cabot asked.

"That's for you to decide when you are older and wiser, Cabot. For now you must respect him."

"He locks Abigail in her room because Videau is in port. He mocks my brother Lawrence's painting. Only one he likes is Thankful, because she has one blue eye and one green, like him. And he won't take me to Ohio with him."

"It's better you're here to look after Hannah. She needs a man around the house."

"Hannah's sweet on you, Captain Lander." Cabot blurted it out then held his breath.

Lander regarded him coolly. "Your sister Hannah may still take it in her head to marry her militia-man."

"Father won't let her. It's *you* she's languishing over."

Lander's eyes narrowed. "Has she told you this?"

"No. But she's said she'll box my ears good if I so much as mention you to her."

"And that means she's sweet on me?"

"She gets flustered if I make mention of you. But then, some people just go about being in love like a mule going up a hill backward. Of course, like everybody else, she's heard talk of the *Prince* and the slave trade. That could be why she won't let me speak of you."

Lander got to his feet abruptly. "I must consult with my workmen. Then we'll walk back to town."

In a few minutes Cabot and Lander were striding on the shoreline, back to the wharves.

"Think," Lander said, "have you ever heard your sister say *anything* nice about me?"

"She told Abby once that there's a rough charm about you. And that lots of girls would give an eye if you'd pay them mind."

Lander grunted. "Let me talk plain. Can I trust you?"

"Yessir."

"I haven't called on Hannah since your father made her turn Louis down. It's because I'm in no position to, yet. A man must have financial means before he sets his cap for a woman. After this venture, I'll have the means."

Cabot mused a bit. "If Hannah knew how you felt, she might wait for you," he ventured.

They walked in silence for a while. Cabot held his breath. Was Lander angry? Perhaps he'd made too bold in speaking out.

"Your father would throw me out the front door," Lander said, "especially with all the talk about the *Prince* and the slave trade."

"That isn't stopping Videau," Cabot reminded

him. "My father won't let him near the house, but he has his plans."

"Plans," Lander said, "yes. A man must always have plans. Look here, Cabot, mayhap you're right and I should speak up."

Cabot glowed inside.

"But I can't divulge the *Prince*'s destination. I'd lose everything. Do you think Hannah would trust me? With all the talk about the *Prince?*"

"It's all she talks about these days," Cabot said, "Trust."

"In what way?"

"Well, it has to do with that quilt she and my other sisters are making. There's to be a piece of fabric in it from everyone who's had to do with our family. Hannah's rules are that there must be trust between such people and us. Or they don't get to be in the quilt."

"Yes, I heard about that," Lander said. "My sister Mattie told me. Lord knows, Hannah and I have known each other all our lives. That should count for something."

He stopped walking. "Thank you, Cabot. You've given me much to think on this day. What will you do with the coin?"

"Buy something special for Hannah."

"Look here, I'm on my way to my mother's shop. Why not stop by with me? She has many pretty notions, some just off incoming ships."

"Thank you, I think I will." Cabot felt happy.

He'd won the gold coin, he'd learned a lot this morning. He had a message for Abby in his pocket that would seal her future. He'd spoken up for Hannah with Captain Lander. He decided he was a true Yankee merchant. He liked profit. And it had been a profitable morning.

Chapter One

March 1788

I remember feeling good about things when I woke up that March morning. I'd managed to keep the peace in our house since January, when my brother Lawrence fought with Father, for giving financial backing to those two Britishers who wanted to start a cotton yarn manufactory in North Beverly.

"Look at what your family did with their dirty mills in England," Lawrence had lashed out at him. As if our father needed reminding. He had come to America in rebellion against his family because of the disease, dependency, and corruption their textile mills had caused there.

It was in January that I hosted a New Year's Day party for the two Britishers. Lawrence sulked, but it did no good. He sulked against Father as Father had sulked against our grandfather. Does it ever end?

No, but I lay in bed that March morning, listening to noises from below stairs and priding myself on the fact that I had kept peace in the house since January. If I didn't, we might all kill each other. Not with guns, no. We'd had our fill of guns with the war. But with words, the way civilized people kill each other every day.

Mattie would be up soon, with my hot chocolate and biscuit. It was 6:30. I lay thinking about Louis, as I did first thing every morning. What was he doing out west now, in the wilderness? Helping to build another fort? Having coffee alone, over a lighted fire on a trail, being watched by an Indian?

The thought of him brought back the sadness and the twinge of guilt. Never a day in my life goes by that I do not feel sadness and guilt about Louis. And wonder if I should have defied my father to marry him and go west.

Louis had written June of '87, proposing to come to Salem and marry me. I could return with him to the Ohio Territory, he'd written. By next spring many families would be migrating out there. Congress was encouraging settlement.

Well, neither Congress nor Louis had taken my father into consideration. Father had refused to allow me to go west. June thirtieth, 1787. I remember the exact date Louis wrote because there was a meteor in the sky at four in the afternoon, bearing over the Isle of Shoals. It was large and appeared to burst, just as I thought my heart would do because Father had said no.

The bitter argument afflicted us both in spirit. Then when it was over and it was decided that I would turn Louis down, the silences between me and Father were even worse.

But I'd managed to keep peace, blessed peace, since January.

That morning in March it was to be shattered.

"Your morning chocolate, Miss Hannah."

Mattie came in with a white pot and cup on a silver tray. The chocolate and biscuit would hold me until breakfast, which was at nine and formal in our house. We all gathered in the dining room to give an accounting to Father of what we would do that day.

I sat up and took the tray. Mattie put a fresh log on the fire. It was cold in the room. The naked branches of the oak tree scraped against my window. As she opened the draperies I could just about see the gray waters of the harbor, anything but calm.

"Any ships due in today?" I asked. If you lived in Salem you kept apprised of such.

"Richard says the *Cheerful Sally* is due from Bordeaux."

Richard Lander was her brother, God help the girl. He's sassy as a codfish aristocrat since my father gave him the *Black Prince* for his own. I'd heard talk that he was fitting out the *Prince* for the slave trade. Well, he always was too big for his britches. And he would get his comeuppance someday.

"It looks cold out there, Mattie."

"It is. I told Cabot to dress warm." She clapped a hand over her mouth.

"So, he's off to the wharves again, is he?"

"Promised he'd be back for breakfast. Don't be hard on him, Miss Hannah. He's after the gold coin from Derby."

She left the room to get warm water so I could wash. I gazed out at the harbor. I thought about Louis again. I'd had only one letter from him since I'd turned him down. He and the small western army were playing leapfrog with the forts they'd constructed up and down the Ohio River, trying to keep up with the settlers who had set down roots illegally. And giving notice to the Indians that the American government intended to protect its people.

I would have gone. Danger or no danger. I wouldn't have been afraid, not with Louis beside me.

Father was going west now. How dangerous could it be? Oh, I could hate my father if I allowed myself to. But I must fight against that or I'd end up an old woman who mumbled to herself. Like Mary Gardner, the widow with all those children who lived behind us.

I would probably end up being an old maid, not even as fortunate as Mary Gardner. I did not mind that. But I would not be bitter or mumble. Nor did I wish to dwell on the "if onlys" of the business.

If only Mama hadn't died when she had Cabot in 1776. Our family would have been so different!

I would have been different, had she lived. Mary Lander, mother of Richard and Mattie, who was also my friend, said that 1776 was the worst year for our family. My father was never the same after that, she said.

If Mama had lived, Cabot wouldn't be the ruffian he was, playing truant from school and running about the wharves. Thankful wouldn't be the spoiled little piece she was. And Abby wouldn't be eloping with that Southerner of hers. And Lawrence, dear Lawrence. I sighed and sipped my hot chocolate.

"You're crying, Miss Hannah."

Mattie came back with the basin of warm water. I wiped away a tear. "I was thinking of Lawrence. He doesn't want to go to Ohio. He wants to stay here and paint portraits. I've been pondering how to convince him the trip will do him good."

She set down the basin of water. "It isn't because of me, Miss Hannah. I've said he should go."

Because of *her*? I stared at the straight-backed figure in the neat skirt, chemise, and starched apron and cap. So it was true, what Abby had told me. Mattie was sweet on our brother Lawrence.

Dear God, this was all we needed! There was no love lost between Father and the Lander family. And hadn't Lawrence fallen far enough from grace with Father, saying he didn't want to be a merchant, wanting to paint portraits, and now not wanting to go to Ohio?

Mattie turned around. Her chin was quivering, her blue eyes filled with tears. Why had I never noticed how pretty she was? Lawrence had noticed it.

"Oh, Miss Hannah, I never intended for it to happen," she said. "It just did. I've told Larry he should go to Ohio. Because we need time away from each other, to think. And he has to prove himself with his father, first."

"*First?*" I couldn't think. I set the bed tray aside, pushed back the covers, reached for my robe, and got up. "Larry? You call him Larry? Only Abby and I call him that."

She started to cry, then. "Oh, don't be angry, please, but I do love him, yes. He's so gentle and dear. But I want what's best for him, please believe me."

She seemed so fragile and appealing and sincere. I hugged her. "Ssh, it's all right, Mattie." I drew back and looked at her. "So, you would marry my brother and be a sister to me, is that it?"

She looked at the floor, gulped, and nodded yes.

I hugged her again. "Well, for myself, I couldn't be more pleased."

"For sure, Miss Hannah?"

"For sure. Only we must keep this from my father, until the right time. And you must call me Hannah, when he is not around."

She smiled.

"And tell me, Mattie. Has Lawrence been behaving himself? He hasn't been bold enough to make free with you, has he?"

Her eyes widened. "Lordy, no. D'you think I haven't been brought up better than that?"

"I know you have. Your dear mama is my best friend. But I also know how charming Lawrence can be."

"Well, he hasn't charmed me that much. Besides which, Richard would kill me."

Ah, yes, Richard, the stern brother. For once I was glad for the way he jealously guarded Mattie.

"He could paint pictures of the Indians," Mattie said suddenly.

"What?"

"Lawrence. He could make their portraits. I mind how you always say you wish you could see what they look like. That time Louis wrote of them. Excuse me for mentioning him, Hannah."

"Why, that's a brilliant idea, Mattie. I'll wager lots of people here in the East would like to know what the Indians in Ohio look like. So many have kin going there."

We smiled at each other. My mind was working fast. This was just the notion that would give Lawrence real purpose in Ohio. Mattie went about her duties and I finished my chocolate and biscuit. While she made the bed, I looked around the room.

Everything about it soothed me, from the crisp white curtains to the walls I'd had papered with the printed liners from China tea chests. I took comfort from the deep window seats, the likeness of Mama that Lawrence had painted from a formal portrait, my books, my pile of fabric I'd collected for our quilt.

"I want a piece of fabric from you for our quilt, Mattie," I said.

She smoothed a blanket over my bed. "You do?"

"Yes. You're part of us. Everyone who has touched our lives and shown trust will have a square in the quilt."

"What color?"

"Red, I think. Your favorite color is red."

"Did you find a piece for your mama's square yet?"

"No. All her clothing was ruined in the storm when we moved here. Blue was her color." I sighed. It had to be the *right* piece of fabric for Mama. She would be the centerpiece of the quilt.

Mattie was getting my warmest woolen dress out. She knew I did errands before breakfast. She laid it on the chair, then looked at me.

"Hannah, I must tell you something."

I waited.

"Your sister Thankful has ordered me to pack her clothing. She says she's going on the Ohio trip with your father and brother."

I groaned. More trouble. "She *wants* to go, Mattie. She isn't. Don't pay her mind."

"I must. She's threatened to tell your pa that she saw me and Lawrence walking together the other evening, if I don't."

"She's threatened you?"

"Yes. And she's threatened to tell him other things, too."

"What other things?"

"Not about me. About others in the family."

I met the blue gaze across the room. *Mattie knows Abby's eloping,* I thought. And somehow Thankful's gotten wind of it. Dear God! I must find out what Thankful knows. And I must be careful not to involve Mattie, lest my father be able to lay blame on her, too, for the elopement.

"Ignore Thankful," I said. "I'll speak to her."

She curtsied and left the room. I sat feeling like a wet woolen cloak had been placed over my shoulders.

Abigail's elopement would cause chaos in the family. And my father's wrath would fall on me when he found out about it. He blamed me for everything that went wrong in the house.

Well, I would be to blame. I was helping Abby and Nate with their plans. I was determined that someone in this family achieve happiness. And I'd gone into it knowing what my father's wrath would be like.

He would say I was trying to kill him. I laughed bitterly. With his disposition, his daily saltwater baths, and vegetarian diet, he would outlive us all.

I sighed. I had been unable to stand up to my father and defy him concerning my own marriage.

Was this why I was helping Abby? Oh, it was too complicated. I did not know.

And now I had another trouble. What to do about Thankful? I had half a mind to ask Father to take her to Ohio. And if she crossed me this week, I would.

I finished my chocolate in a gulp, washed, and dressed quickly. Suddenly the pleasant room stifled me. I must walk in the fresh, saltwater morning air. It always restored me. I would go to the wharf and visit Mary Lander in her shop. I would bring sweet buns and we would have tea.

I could no longer bear the family's problems alone. I slipped down the back stairs and out the door, cut through my garden to inspect some crocuses and daffodils, which were already shooting up through the muddy ground. I couldn't wait to work in my flower garden again. Oh, the fog was lifting, the sun was coming up. It promised to be a lovely day.

Chapter Two

I crossed Derby Street and walked onto Derby Wharf. My spirits lifted. I loved the bustle of the wharf, early mornings, the smells of coffee, tea, cloves. So much noise, what with creaking windlasses from ships, men shouting, and the pounding and sawing from nearby shipyards. I stepped into a bakery and purchased some sweet buns, then walked the short distance to Mary Lander's shop.

"How did you know I just put up the water for tea?" she asked as the bell rang and I came through the door.

"I always know, Mary."

In minutes we were sipping tea at the scarred oak table in the corner. I loved her shop, with its shelves of shoes and pots, its baskets and staves of tea, coffee, sugar, and fruit, its piles of textiles, bags of spices, and notions.

We talked of the upcoming party I was giving for Father's departure to Ohio. "Of course, Lawrence still doesn't want to go," I said.

"It's my Mattie who's been bedeviling him," she allowed.

"She loves him, Mary. But she's not trying to keep him here. She even suggested that he do portraits of the Indians. She's been most helpful."

"Then what's plaguing you, Hannah?" she asked. "If not that my girl is smitten with your brother."

I sighed. "Thankful has ordered Mattie to start packing her clothes. She wants to go on the Ohio trip. She threatens that she'll tell she saw Mattie and Lawrence walking together, if I don't let her go!"

"The child needs a good whipping," Mary said.

"She needs something, Mary. She's terribly wicked, because Father coddles her so. I'm tempted to ask him to take her."

A glint came into Mary's eyes. "And why not?" she asked. "It's just the thing. Do the little chit some good. You can't control her anymore, Hannah. She's gotten the best of you too often. She's wild and unruly. Nothing in Salem satisfies her."

I bit my lip. "Wouldn't that be giving up with her?"

"*Give* up with her, Hannah!" she urged. "The child has run you ragged. She won't do her chores, has to be dragged to your quilting sessions, then does all her stitches wrong and you have to redo them. She torments poor Cabot. My Mattie has told me. And she hates dame school, you know that."

I nodded. "But I'd be disappointing Mama, giving up with Thankful."

She put her hand on mine on the table. "She's your father's responsibility, not yours. You're only sixteen, child."

"I feel like an old woman sometimes."

"He puts too much on you, that father of yours."

"Why can't I make Thankful mind? Why is she so wicked?"

"It's the one blue eye and the one green," Mary said. "It's the Devil's grip on them both. She's just like him. Let him worry about her."

"I brood on it, Mary."

"You brood too much for one so young."

"I have my reasons."

"Louis?" she asked carefully.

I felt myself blushing. "Sometimes, Mary, I think I should have defied Father and said yes to Louis. What if he never comes back and I never see him again?"

She set her tea cup down. Her face was all wrinkles, but she wore them like lace, with pride. "Did it ever occur to you, Hannah Chelmsford, that if Louis really loved you, he'd wait?"

I just stared at her. It never had.

"And that there might be other fish in the sea?"

"Oh, Mary, I'm so muddle-headed, I can't think on that now. My sister is eloping with Nate next week, the night of my father's party. I've had a hand in her elopement. That's all I can think of at the moment."

She was surprised at the news, but accepting. " 'Tis a shame she has to elope. But your father has driven her to it. I've known that girl since she was born. And I've had business dealings with Nate. He's forthright as rain. And not afraid of sailing into the wind. Abby is bright as brass and she'll sail into the wind with him."

"Then I haven't done wrong, helping them?"

"If this happens on your watch, you've done well. Your mother would be pleased. Now, what can I do to help with the wedding?"

I breathed easier. "I won't be able to be there. I'd be beholden if you'd stand up for Abby in my place."

"I'll be there, Hannah. And I'll make the wedding cake."

I was about to leap out of my chair and hug her when the doorbell tinkled and someone came in.

"Cabot!" Why did it not surprise me to see him with Richard Lander? I ignored Lander, uneasy in his presence. We'd been in each other's company only twice since last summer. And never alone.

"Have you been playing the wharf rat again?" I scolded my brother.

"He's been with me," Richard said. "We wharf rats have to hang together." He took off his jacket, headed for the tea kettle on the hearth, poured a cup, and gave it to Cabot.

"Don't scold. Your brother got the gold coin from Derby."

"Nate figured her arrival time." Cabot sipped his tea and showed me the coin. "And he gave me a note for Abigail."

"Well, heavens, deliver it then and be careful." I looked up to see Richard, outlined against the panes of curtainless windows, amid barrels and stacks of textiles. He was smiling at me. I drew in my breath, remembering things I preferred to forget. And he knew it, too. His blue eyes bore into me, seeing my soul.

I gripped the rough wool of Cabot's coat. "Go and deliver the note and be ready for breakfast."

"I wanted to buy something for you with my coin."

"That's sweet, but not today. Come back another time. Mary will help you."

Mary nodded and smiled at him. He set his cup down, said goodbye, and left. Then the three of us sat in awkward silence. The fire crackled. From outside came the rumble of wagon wheels on the wharf, the banging of hammers, the shouts of men.

"Your father always said fortune favors the bold," Richard said. "Nate is bold and he gets the girl."

"Cabot shouldn't have shared that note with you."

"He didn't. Nate's asked me to stand up for him at the wedding."

Both Mary and I expressed surprise.

"It's an honor I'll perform gladly," Richard said.

"It's good to see those two follow the course set by their hearts. I hope they have a good wind behind them, always."

I stood up. "I must go, Mary." I hugged her. "Thank you for the tea and the advice." I turned to Richard. "There are some who cannot follow the course set by their hearts. It is a luxury they cannot afford."

"Or, mayhap, they're off course and don't know it," he said.

The cheek! He was speaking of Louis! Saying I was off course loving him. And he was intimating other things that I preferred not to think of.

I said nothing. I nodded at Mary who was eyeing the two of us, sensing things now. I would have some explaining to do to Mary if I did not leave soon. I went out the door. But Richard followed.

He offered a hand under my elbow. I shook him off. He smiled, extended both hands, palms up, in a gesture of peace. Then he fell into step with me. "Do you mind if I walk a ways with you?"

"Suit yourself. Although I would prefer not to be seen in the company of the owner of a slave ship."

"I'm hurt sore that you think such of me, Hannah."

"What am I to think, with all the talk? I'm sorry for what my father did to your father, Richard. When you told me of it, I was ashamed. And if I could make it up to you, I would. But using the

Prince for a slave ship is a shabby way to get back at my family."

He stopped walking. "In heaven's name, Hannah, I thought you would not be one to be pulled into the gossip. And know that secrecy is of the utmost importance in this venture."

"I've lived here since I was a child, Richard. Never have I known such secrecy to be attached to a voyage."

"You could trust me, then." It was said with sadness. But at the same time it angered me.

"What have you done that I should?"

"I've done everything I said I would. I've kept all my promises to you. This voyage is the last part of those promises. I intend to return the *Prince* to her true glory."

"Richard." I groped for words.

"I need a year, Hannah, to keep the last of my promises. Will you wait for me a year?"

Dear God, this wasn't possible. He wasn't going to bring up *that* old business again. "For what?" My heart hammered.

"For me to clear Salem Harbor under my own merchant's banner, put into foreign ports with what's in my hold, strike my deals, and bring home my cargo."

He was looking at me hopefully. "I certainly shall wait to see what surprises you have in store for us, Richard."

"I'm not asking you to wait for that."

"For what, then? Say it plain."

"I said it plain once, Hannah."

My face flamed. "Richard, that was so long ago! We're not even friends anymore. You've traveled the world. I've been betrothed. Since you're home, you've kept your distance."

"There was Louis." His voice was grave. "For all I know, there may still be Louis."

"There is no more Louis," I said softly. "He loves the west too much. And I've hurt him grievously."

He nodded. "I've been working and scrambling to get money to get the *Prince* seaworthy, since I heard you turned Louis down. I've been planning this venture. And getting investors. So I could have something in hand to offer you."

I struggled for words. My mind was whirling. "We don't *know* each other anymore, Richard."

"You still have feelings for me. I saw them in your eyes before, in my mother's shop. Be honest with yourself for once, Hannah. Think why you turned Louis down."

"My father . . ." I began.

"No." He was smiling. It irritated me. "You'd have gone against your father if you really wanted to go west with Louis. You're going against his wishes for Abby."

I was becoming angry. "Speak plain then, since you know so much."

"You turned Louis down because you're a Salem lady, born and bred. Not a frontier woman. I might add, you're a spoiled Salem lady. Your comforts mean too much to you."

"How dare you?" My face went red.

He laughed. "You said speak plain. Let me finish then."

"Do."

"You are not a frontier woman, Hannah." He was solemn. "You need the salt smell of the sea, as I do. And a grand house in a port town. You'd die without the sea."

"I loved Louis." My voice cracked.

"You loved the freedom you saw in him. The freedom from your father that going west would have allowed you."

I had no answer for that.

"I'll build you a grander house than any in Salem, Hannah. You can bring Cabot to live with us. I'll educate him for the sea. Do you want him to be a wharf rat forever?"

"Leave Cabot out of this, Richard."

He shook his head no. "There's no leaving him out of it. I know how much he means to you. But he is part of why you couldn't go west. There's no sin in it, Hannah. But don't lie to yourself. If you loved Louis enough, you'd throw over everything here in a moment, as Abigail is doing."

I commenced to walk away from him. "It was my father who kept me from Louis," I insisted.

"Then you should take example from Abigail and chart your course away from him. As from a hurricane."

"I'd be going into the eye of the hurricane, marrying you."

"You've the spirit for it."

I whirled toward him. His blue eyes were serene, not combative. He meant every word he said.

"Will you wait for me?" he asked softly.

People were pushing past us on the busy wharf as we stood staring at each other. "You haven't said anything about love."

He glanced around. "Here?"

"You've said everything else here."

"All right, Hannah Chelmsford. I love you. Would I be putting myself through this if I didn't? I'd rather ride out the perils of the sea."

"Prove you love me."

"How?"

"Oh, I wouldn't ask you to do anything *romantic*, Richard Lander. Prove it by telling me the true destination of the *Prince*. I'll keep a still tongue in my head."

His face went white. He held up his hands again. "I can't. I've sworn secrecy to my investors. I'm not in this alone."

"Then we remain friends and no more," I said, moving along the busy wharf. "I wish you well in your venture."

"Hannah." His voice was low and compelling. I turned. He stood there, hands on his hips. "I'll take you with me on the maiden voyage of the *Prince*. We'll sail the coast, if you want romance, before I clear the harbor with my cargo. It'll all be proper. I'll bring my sister along. But I can't divulge my destination."

I took his measure. He struck a fine figure of a man standing there. Determined, confident, and Lord knew he was capable. "You still don't understand," I said. "I'm not sure I do myself. Or if I can put it into words."

"Try."

"I want trust, Richard. I've had romance. Louis was the dearest. But it wasn't enough to get me to go west. Perhaps you are right. Perhaps I didn't love Louis enough to give up all I have. But that means I couldn't give him my trust."

I looked at him beseechingly, begging him to understand. He nodded. I went on. "Lack of trust ruined my parents' marriage. Which makes me think I'll never be able to give it, either. So it's become more precious to me. I'll anchor my next love with it, Richard. If there *is* a next love. But the trust will have to be on both sides."

He looked sad.

"You know, we're making a quilt now, my sisters and I. At first there were only supposed to be pieces in it for family. Then I told my sisters we should have a piece in it for everyone who's ever meant anything to us in our lives. But the rules are that there must have been trust between such people and us. That makes people family."

He smiled wryly. "Seems to me you're trying to

piece your life together with this quilt, Hannah."

"Mayhap you're right, Richard. Mayhap I am. It needs piecing."

"Will I get to be a part of the quilt?"

"I don't know yet, Richard. I'm still deciding if some people will be in it. If I decide to let you in, I'll ask you for some fabric that had to do with your life."

"Are there any rules as to the kind of fabric?"

"No, but I wouldn't worry the matter now."

He bowed. "I shall bring a piece back from my voyage."

I left him standing there, staring after me. I felt his eyes boring into my back. Tears crowded my own eyes as I pushed past people. My legs were unsteady and my heart was racing. He brought back so much that I hadn't known still lived inside me. Feelings surfaced, as if at high tide, and threatened to pull me into their undertow. I felt drowned in them as I rushed away.

Chapter Three

By the time I arrived at my back door my head was spinning with one thought only.

Richard Lander had asked me to marry him.

It was the third time in my life. The first time I had been four and he ten.

In the back hall I took off my wrap. No one was about, though I did hear noise from the kitchen. I went into the sun-filled dining room. Margaret had laid the table for breakfast. At the sideboard I poured a cup of tea from the silver pot, pulled a small rocker in front of the blazing hearth, and sat down, cup in lap. I was shaking. I took a moment to look around the room. The pristine whiteness of the sheer curtains, the polished, wide, floorboards covered by the Turkish carpet, the table laid for breakfast with crystal and china, all gave me heart. Perhaps Richard is right, I thought. Perhaps I need my surroundings here to frame my life, to contain my fears, to give substance to my beliefs, or I will go mad.

I did not know where everyone else was. I did

not care. I sipped the hot brew, savoring the precious quiet moments. Allowing myself to think back on all that had happened and how it used to be.

Seldom did I allow myself that luxury. Who knew what passions I would let loose? How long now did Richard and I know each other? I counted back. It was 1775. Lawrence was six that year, Abigail two, Thankful a baby of four months, and Cabot not yet born.

The British were in Boston. My father was away, captaining one of his ships to bring supplies to the American army that besieged Boston, keeping the British penned in there. Sometimes my father smuggled Patriot refugees out.

Other British had come ashore in Salem to purchase goods. It was the end of May. Their warships were offshore, an offense to the eyes, a blot on the horizon. I remember everyone in town pointing to them, fearfully.

I was too young to know the why of it, but some British came into our old house across town. I remember them sitting at the dining room table, and Mama serving them. From across the room I stared at their polished boots, their swords and sashes, their tricorn hats. I remember being surprised that they ate and spoke just like us. I'd been terrified when they first came to the house, but then everything was all right.

One of them, the very tall one, took me on his knee and showed me his gold pocketwatch. He explained that the pretty design on the back was his family crest. And then they all went outside. They wanted more wine. I remember my mother pointing the way to the root cellar.

They did not come back inside. If I thought about it at all, I suppose I thought they were having a fine time of it out there, drinking my father's wine.

We children were sent to bed.

A few days later, the one who'd shown me his watch came back. It was evening and Lawrence and Abigail and I and baby Thankful were already in bed. But I got up and peeked through the banister as our maidservant let him in. All I could see were his boots and part of his blue naval officer's coat. But I knew his voice. Then I went back to bed.

There was a bad storm that night. But between its rumblings I heard the British officer's voice downstairs in our parlor. It was a nice voice, soothing. I was glad to hear a man's voice down there. The storm had frightened me and I missed my father.

Next morning the sun was out and the officer was gone and Mary Lander was at our breakfast table. That's when I met Richard and his sister Mattie, who was a year younger than me. I asked my mother why the British officer had left. She said he'd never come back, that I must have been dreaming.

I know I hadn't dreamed it. But it didn't matter,

because my mother's eyes and face were red. She'd been crying. And Mary Lander was very tender with her, talking with her in the fragments of language grownups use when children are present. So the words make no sense to the children, but the grownups understand.

Mary Lander came over almost every day to be with my mother after that. And Richard and I became friends. My father came home at the end of June. And he was very angry at the British.

They had set fire to Charlestown. He spoke, in reverent tones, about a place called Bunker Hill. He seemed changed. No longer did he laugh or play with us. He pushed us aside, scolded when we made too much noise, and he and my mother did not speak anymore at the supper table.

Lawrence said Father was angry with Mother for allowing the British in our house.

Richard said that my mother had captured the British. "She invited them in to eat," he told us, "then sent them to the root cellar to fetch more wine. Then she closed the door on them and locked them in and called the local militia. And they were placed under arrest. But set free."

My father went away again in July. All summer, he was cruising the *Black Prince* in and out of New England's harbors, Richard told me, eluding the British, to get provisions to the American army around Boston.

Richard told me how some townspeople had

stopped talking to my mother because she'd fed the British. It didn't matter that she'd captured them, he said. She'd let them in the house. That's all people would remember. So my mother was tainted with the same brush as town merchants who'd sold them provisions.

I minded how sad it made my mother. But she had one friend, Mary Lander, who came every day.

About the time that Cabot was born, in February of '76, Mary Lander and her children started staying overnight. She had to. Because Mama died within a day or so of Cabot's birth and there was a houseful of children to care for. And the maidservant quit.

I thought my world had ended. I remember how it was when the midwife left and Mary Lander came to tell Lawrence and me and Abigail that our mother was dead. She hugged us and we cried. It was raining outside, a cold relentless rain. And my father was away. I never felt so abandoned. If not for Richard, who never left my side all day, I think I would have died.

Mama was laid out in the parlor and people came in to pay their respects. "My mother shouldn't let them in," Richard said. "They're the ones who wouldn't talk to your mother because she fed the British."

But Mary Lander let them in, took the food they brought, laid it out in the dining room, and they all sat around and talked about the war and made clucking sounds of sadness when they looked at us children who had to sit on the sidelines in our best clothing and stay quiet.

That was when Richard asked me to marry him. "I'll always take care of you," he said.

I agreed. It seemed like a good arrangement.

Lawrence and Richard slept in the same room. And before we went to bed at night in the room we shared, they allowed Mattie and Abigail and me to come to their room and listen to the ghost stories they told. Most times Mattie would fall asleep. Richard told wonderful ghost stories! He said one of his ancestors had been hanged as a witch back in 1692 and now haunted the town. When I asked Mary the next day she said yes, it was true.

She was able to stay because her husband was a ship's captain, and away a lot.

Then in March 1776, when Cabot was only a month old and we were sitting around telling ghost stories, Richard waited for Mattie to fall asleep. When she dutifully did, he told us something more frightening than any ghost story.

He said his father had shot himself, a week ago.

Lawrence and I didn't know what to say. Abby was too young to understand. But I knew it was true, or Richard wouldn't have said it. Next day I stayed very close to Mary Lander as she went about caring for our household. I helped her with the chores. She was dry-eyed and stoic. She said not to worry, she wouldn't leave us.

I thought the world was going to pieces around me. Both my mother and Richard's father were dead. I thought our household was cursed by the witch that was Richard's ancestor. I was a child growing up in war. It formed my whole world. I considered tragedy the natural order of things. Richard and I became closer because of it. I looked to him for comfort.

Then, one day in June, my father came home. And he brought Margaret with him.

There had been a battle. With the *Black Prince* Father had helped to capture two British transports in Plymouth Harbor. They were carrying the 71st Highland Regiment and their families. They were out of Glasgow, Scotland, Boston bound, not realizing that British General Howe had evacuated Boston in March.

More death. Several Highlanders were killed in the battle. Father helped bury Margaret's husband in the sands off Long Island and brought her home to take care of us.

I cried so when Mary Lander left us. Father offered her money for her services, but she refused. "I did it for Sara," she said of my mother. It seemed that she and my father did not like each other very much.

After that, Father did not want us to see Mary anymore. And he would not mention Mother's name. It was banished from the house, except when he chose to chide one of us for some wrongdoing, to say we'd turn out like her if we weren't careful.

I sneaked out to see Mary and Richard. She was the last tie I had with my mother. What had Mother done that was so wrong, I'd ask Mary. "It's the war and what it's done to your father," she'd say. Sometimes I brought Abby and baby Cabot. Father had no interest in Cabot. Fortunately, Father was away most of the war. Margaret understood. She allowed it. She even sent me with special dishes she'd cooked. And so it was that Margaret and I became friends.

Richard grew up fast after his father died. He seemed to turn, overnight, from a laughing boy into a grave-eyed young man, at eleven. We played about the wharves and he took me with him when he helped his mother in her store. He looked after his little sister. He took Mattie and me and Abby to see the fort being built out of old hulks and timbers to block Salem's northern harbor for defense of the town. Every time a privateer came into port with her hold filled with British booty, every time a British "prize" ship docked, manned by Americans who had captured her, we were there.

Children of war, we grew up fast. Childhood was foreshortened. Before the war ended, when he was fifteen, Richard went into my father's counting house.

"I won't be able to see you much anymore," he said. "I'll be too busy, serving my apprenticeship.

Then I'll be a captain's clerk. Then I'll sign on one of your father's ships. I'll captain my own ship someday. Then we'll marry."

It seemed the natural order of things. I said yes once again. It was 1780 and I was eight.

In the next year I saw Richard only in the company of my father, when Abby and I visited the counting house or we brought gifts to Mary Lander's house at Christmas. Richard was growing fast into a man. He was formal and polite, but distant. I know he hated my father. But I did not know why.

He learned naval architecture from some elderly seamen in the counting house. And he did sign onto one of my father's ships, soon as the war ended, when he was sixteen. When I went to the wharf to see him off, surrounded by so many others, he drew me aside for a moment. And that was when he told me that his father had taken the blame for my father going against the Continental Congress's regulations. And how his father was ruined and killed himself.

"I'll always hate him," he told me.

"But he's educated you and given you your chances," I said.

"To ease his own conscience. And make himself look good in the eyes of Salem town."

He cleared Salem Harbor on one of my father's ships. He said no more about marrying me. I was so stunned by what he'd told me about my father that I consigned that promise to where it belonged.

Back in my childhood. I was only nine, but no longer a child. With Mama gone, I personally took charge of the little ones.

My father's fleet was down to two ships after the war, not counting the *Prince*, which was ruined and in dry dock. Richard was away at sea a lot in the next few years. He saved one of my father's ships from being captured by pirates once, and my father made him a midshipman.

He sailed to many foreign ports and came home looking taller each time. And browned and stern-looking. He never came to our house to call. Fall of 1786 he cleared Salem Harbor for the West Indies and was gone until the following spring.

In Philadelphia, at my father's brother's house, where Abby and I were visiting, I met Louis.

It was Christmas, 1786. I was fifteen, Louis was the second son in a good family. Partly to prove himself to his father, who was a Revolutionary War hero, and partly for the excitement of it, he'd joined the Pennsylvania Militia. He was on leave from the Northwest Territory, where he was serving under Captain Walter Finney, helping to build new forts and protecting the frontier.

He was a guest of my Aunt Ann and Uncle Phillip. He'd earned the leave, but he was also back to recruit new men.

He was twenty. And different. I'd never met anyone like Louis. He was handsome, yes, and browned and muscled, from his exertions out west. And when he wore his fringed frontier clothes to the dances Aunt Ann gave, to attract new recruits, he said, I knew only that I wanted to be standing next to him. To dance with him. And when he told stories about the Ohio Territory and the Indian attacks and how the militia had floated fifty-ton galleys two hundred miles downstream from the little village of Pittsburgh to protect the new settlers, my mind took flight.

I felt my narrow world blossoming around Louis. I began to realize there was a whole way of life outside the confines of Salem, with its grim-faced codfish aristocrats who never smiled and lived by rules set down a hundred and fifty years ago.

In contrast, Louis's world had no constrictions. It was limitless with possibilities. Its rivers were new and clean, its forests abundant with game and timber, its rules made up as the people went along.

Perhaps Richard was right in what he'd said. Perhaps Louis and everything he stood for represented a freedom to me that I'd never before dreamed about. Louis was easy in his dealings with people, expansive in everything he did. His hopes were as limitless as the unchartered land. He laughed a lot. Life was a joy, an adventure.

Nobody I'd known in Salem had ever been like that.

With Father's permission I extended our Philadelphia visit. With Father's permission, we became betrothed. I'm sure Father never dreamed Louis would ask me to go west. Abby gave me moral support. Bubbly and outgoing herself, she adored Louis, too. But she would never go west, she said. She'd marry a sea captain and see the world.

It was January of 1787. We received word from Father that Lawrence and a force of over 4,000 Massachusetts militiamen had been called up to put down Shay's Rebellion.

Louis assured us Lawrence would be fine. Lawrence wrote and congratulated me on my betrothal. Louis and I made plans. He would go back to the Ohio wilderness and when Congress opened up the territory to settlers and it was safe for women to be brought out, he would come back and we would marry. We would start a new world. I did not keep my plans from Father. I ponder that he was just too busy to pay mind.

Father came to fetch us in Philadelphia, bringing the younger children. He met Louis, who went back with his new recruits just before we all returned to Salem. I had a singing heart. When Richard came home in the spring, my father gave him the *Prince*. Richard kept busy with the ship and I was busy finishing up decorating our fine new home, which we'd just moved into a year earlier.

That June the *Swamp Fox* dropped anchor in Salem, and Abby met her sea captain and fell in love. Father started to pay mind. He was furious and he started to act strange. It was as if something evil was loosed in him.

When Louis's letter came that same month, asking me to set the date and come west the next spring, Father said no. What was happening to his daughters, he said? Were they becoming like their mother? I didn't know what he meant and I fought him. But did I fight him hard enough? I ponder, in the light of what Richard said earlier, that I could have fought harder.

Oh, I know now that the plans Louis and I made that Christmas were not feasible. But not because I love my home in Salem too much. It was because, by last June, when Louis wrote, I had become sensible of the fact that my family was broken into pieces.

Things were dreadfully wrong.

Father forbade Abby ever to see Nate or write to him, again. But they corresponded and Nate returned before the end of the year. Father kept hinting dreadful things to me and Abby about Mama, and how Abby would end up just like her.

He was angry with Lawrence, who, back from his stint with the militia and the rebellion, had a new sense of purpose and was saying he did not want to follow my father's footsteps and become a Salem merchant. He wanted to paint portraits. Mama had done watercolors. Father forbade it. There was a weakness in our family, he said, and it came from our mother.

There was a terrible undercurrent in our house, of secrets, that flowed from my father's mind and threatened to poison us all. And as we started to grow up and make plans, he acted as if we were turning on him.

Then Cabot started to run free at the wharves, playing truant from school, making friends with ships' masters. I feared he would run away. He and Thankful fought constantly. She was becoming more and more unruly and Father always took up for her. And gave Cabot the rough side of his tongue. One would think he enjoyed setting them against one another.

No, I could not marry Louis and go west and leave this poor broken family. I had to try to put it together again. Why had that thought never occurred to Richard?

Why had it never occurred to me until now?

Oh, Louis! Forgive me.

It was about last fall that I started the idea for the quilt. Perhaps Richard was right about that, anyway. Perhaps doing it is my way of piecing our lives back together again.

Chapter Four

"Sure'n if you don't do something about that girrle, I dinna know if I'll be stayin' on in this house!"

Margaret came into the dining room. She still spoke with the accent of a Scottish Highlander. I looked up to see her standing in the doorway, ample in build, round of face, and purposeful.

"What has Thankful done now?"

"She pounced on Cabot the minute he shows his head in the door this mornin', demandin' to know where he was. Next thing I know they're rollin' on the floor like two bairns without any upbringin', and he's runnin' after her to get back a note."

"What note?"

"How would I be knowin' that?"

"Where is Cabot?"

"In his room."

He was on his bed, crying. A large bruise was swelling on his forehead. "Cabot!" I sat next to him on the bed.

He was shivering and would not look at me. "She's taken the note. She knows what's in it. She says she's going to tell Father."

Dear God.

"I'm no account," he was saying. "Can't even deliver a note to Abby."

"You listen to me, Cabot. You are not no account. You've delivered many a note to Abby. And we'll get this one to her, too, without Father knowing what's in it."

He raised his tear-filled eyes to mine.

"Now do as I say. Go wash and appear at breakfast as if nothing's happened. If Father asks you what happened, say you fell."

He wiped his nose with his sleeve. "Thank you, Hannah. But how will you stop her from telling?"

I did not know how. I told him I would think of something, then left the room. I was somewhat afraid of my little sister Thankful. I sensed something evil in her at thirteen.

Something there was about the one blue eye and the one green that rendered her gaze too like my father's. She became more like him every day. Of late she'd even started shunning meat and eating only vegetables, as he did. And she was more practiced in feminine wiles than I or Abby.

She was no longer a child. Perhaps she never had been, I minded as I knocked on her door.

"You may enter, Hannah."

She was ensconced on the window seat. Her room overlooked the harbor. It was the room

Cabot had wanted, but she had gotten it. She smiled sweetly as I entered. On the brown wool of her skirt, she held some fabric of a deep, rich blue.

"You've come to scold, no doubt. Well, do it and be done with it. Heavens, it's your sisterly duty, Hannah."

She was two-faced, as well. She could feign an attitude of sweetness that always beguiled me and made me feel that perhaps the fault was mine, perhaps I misunderstood her.

"Give me the note," I said.

"Oh, that?" She gestured to it. "It's there on the floor. You may have it."

"Pick it up and hand it to me."

"Oh, yes. I must allow you to hold sway over me as mistress of the house. Very well, I promised Father I would." She set the blue fabric aside, slid off the window seat, retrieved the note, and held it just beyond my reach.

"*Give it to me*," I ordered.

Her laughter was like birdsong. "Oh, Hannah, don't be tiresome. You'll get frown lines if you take life so seriously."

"I suppose you'll be running to Father with what you've learned here."

She laughed again. "No. I intend to use it to bargain with. Give me what I want, and I don't breathe a word to Father."

From somewhere in the house I heard a door slam, then the sound of Father's voice, then Lawrence's. Then strange voices. Dear God, he'd brought guests for breakfast! In the sunlight that streamed in the window, Thankful's reddish hair gleamed. Her eyes were innocence itself.

"What do you want?"

"I want to go to Ohio with Father. He'll take me if you ask him to. I want to be with him, not left here at home. Convince him and I'll keep a still tongue in my head. Abby could be running off with Elias Hasket Derby and I wouldn't say anything."

I had to gather my wits. I knew I was not in a strong position. This child-woman had outwitted me. I must protect Abby. And what did I care if Thankful went to Ohio? I was well rid of her. She kept the household in turmoil and I knew I wouldn't be able to control her once Father left.

"The trip won't be easy," I said.

"That's exactly why I want to go. For the adventure of it. What sport is there here? School? I hate it. I hate needlework, French, and dancing lessons. I'll be better company for Father than that fop Lawrence."

"Your brother is not a fop and you know it."

"You're right, I'm sorry. He's smitten with Mattie. There's something else I could tell Father."

That decided me. "All right, you win, I'll ask him."

"When?"

"As soon as I can."

"You must do it today. So I can be packed in time."

"You will be packed in time, Thankful." I turned to leave the room. "I promise."

She handed me the note.

"Oh, Hannah." She caught my arm. "I meant to give you this, wait." She picked up the blue fabric. "I found this in the attic in an old trunk. You could use it for Mama's piece of the quilt."

I took the fabric. It was wool, very soft, of deep blue in color. It looked like part of a coat. But the sleeves were missing. I unfolded it. A man's coat! The facing was also missing. I felt a strange thrill, holding it.

"Whose is it?" I asked.

"Perhaps Father's. From the war."

It had some gold braid on it. And so many lovely buttonholes. "It's a man's coat, all right. Military. From the Revolution. But the fabric for Mama's piece of the quilt should be something of hers. Something she wore."

"Oh, come, Hannah, you know Father threw everything of hers out."

I stared at my sister. Father had told the rest of us that all Mama's clothing had been ruined by rain in the move to our new house. Thankful met my eyes, a peculiar smile on her face. And so then it was that I knew it to be true. *Father had thrown Mother's things out.* And he had told Thankful.

I nodded. My mouth was dry. "Perhaps it was

part of the booty Father captured when he was privateering," I said.

"Yes, I'm sure it is. And Mother was intending to make something of it. You told me how she was always sewing and couldn't bear to waste anything."

I nodded. During the war fabric had been scarce. Perhaps Mama had wanted to make something for Lawrence out of it. "I suppose we could stretch the rules for the quilt a bit," I mused. "It must have meant something to Mama that she kept it."

"Yes." And she reached for it. "Here, I'll take it downstairs and put it in the back parlor for you."

I relinquished the fabric. Thankful's face had suddenly assumed a sweetness that made her seem like a different person. Perhaps this trip to Ohio will be a good thing for her, I minded. "We'll have our usual quilting session after breakfast," I said.

"All right, Hannah," she said meekly.

Usually I had to drag her to our quilting session. I sighed. Perhaps I could salvage something from this day after all.

Abby's room was on the third floor and the stairway to the widow's walk was in the middle of it. She had made a special place for herself up there.

"Oh, Hannah!" She hugged me when she read the note. "We'll be married before we clear Salem Harbor. Think on it!"

I hugged her slender frame. She was still in her

dressing gown, her tawny-colored hair about her shoulders. Her blue eyes danced with light. I felt a stab of pain in my heart. Abigail was the prettiest of us all. Though slender, she was round in all the right places, where I feared that I was all angles. And a bubbling happiness emerged from her like from a mountain spring.

"Yes, it's all set," I said. "But are you *sure*, Abby, that this is what you want?"

"Oh." And she danced around the room. "I am, Hannah, I am. Come up the stairs and I'll show you something."

I followed her up the stairs to the widow's walk. Here, you could see all of Salem town and harbor.

"Look," she pointed. "There. The *Swamp Fox*."

I looked and smiled at her.

"Nate and I have a system of signals. A red flag on the foremast means there will be a note today. A blue one means he's about town seeing to his cargo. A white one means look through the telescope. There was a red one this morning. And look." She pointed to a pair of lace-trimmed drawers she had attached to the knob of an open window. "That means I await his message."

"Abby! That's scandalous!"

She giggled. "They catch the wind better than any other piece of clothing. When a white flag appears and I look through the telescope, he stands on the quarterdeck and flashes written signs at me. Like broadsides. Sometimes they say 'I love you.' Oh, Hannah, I'm having so much fun. Father thinks he's got me confined up here. But I'm sewing my trousseau and packing."

"What are those ropes?" Attached to a hook outside the widow's walk was a stout rope, the kind used on a ship.

"Why, Hannah, every night after dark I lower down a packet of my things. Clothing or books or mementos I want to take with me. How else could I get my possessions aboard?" Her blue eyes widened.

"Oh, Abby, you're really going." I hugged her again.

"Yes, isn't it exciting? Oh, I thank you so for helping to get the preacher. But why did you bring the note just now and not Cabot?"

"Thankful intercepted him."

She drew back, aghast. "She knows?"

"Yes, but don't worry. She wanted something from me to keep from telling. She was bargaining. I gave her what she wanted."

"What?"

"She wants me to convince Father to take her to Ohio."

"And you'll do it?"

"Yes, Abby. The child does want to go. Why not? She hates it here. I can't control her. And she had me cornered like a fox this morning."

"The she-devil!" Then she brightened. "Well, mayhap it's all for the best. At least you won't have her plaguing you anymore. *Now* what, Hannah? What else is bothering you?"

I sat on the top step of the widow's walk and she sat next to me. "I fear your being at sea," I confessed. "What kind of life is that for a woman?"

"A marvelous life," she mused dreamily.

"What is Nate's destination?"

"Lisbon, to the West Indies. Probably all of the windward islands in the Caribbean. Then to Charleston."

"But, Abby, how will you live on a ship for so many months?"

"Hannah, stop fussing. Many captains' wives travel on trading vessels. Nate says that soon anyone of consequence in Salem will have been around the world at least once."

"That doesn't becalm me, Abby."

"Very well. Nate has a wonderful captain's cabin. It has alcoves fitted with a settle, windows protected by heavy shutters, and a skylight. The *Swamp Fox* was built for both speed and strength. It's armed with small cannon. Our stateroom has its own privy that draws either salt or fresh water. And a medicine chest with everything in it. The furniture is richly upholstered. The sideboard is teak. We even have Persian carpets. Of course, they have to be stowed while we sail. But I'll take them out when we drop anchor. And all the furniture is bolted down to hold my things in place. I'll take my good tea set, my laces and linens."

"I suppose you'll be doing the cooking and washing."

"For shame, Hannah! Why a captain's wife is royalty, aboard a trader. I'll be coddled to death. Merlin does the cooking and he's better than our Margaret."

I nodded. "But you'll be the only woman aboard."

"Not true, though if it were, Nate would care for me. Merlin's wife came this trip. And she's offered to be my personal maid. Nate's bringing a goat aboard, so I'll have fresh milk. And he *always* has fresh fruits and vegetables for his crew."

I contemplated all this, nodding.

"Oh, Hannah, I'll be so happy. I'll have all the time I want to read and study, play cribbage, and write in my journal. Nate's going to teach me to read the compass, too. And I'll work on my part of the quilt. You will let me take it?"

"Of course." I wanted to cry. Abby was so full of life, so fearless. Like Mary had said, she was as bright as brass and not afraid of sailing into the wind.

She made me feel colorless and wan by comparison.

"Good," she said. "I'll be meeting people and mayhap I can make friends and add a few more pieces to my part of the quilt. Oh, Hannah, I do want to meet people! I want to see the world. Canton and the Sandwich Islands! Lisbon! I want to swim the blue water of the West Indies. And I'll sail back into Salem Harbor someday soon, don't worry." She hugged me. "Do you feel better now?"

"Yes, if all you say is true."

"It is. Stop by and see the *Swamp Fox* one day this week. Nate will be glad to see you again. Ask him to let you see our stateroom." She blushed. "Be happy for me, Hannah. You remember how beautiful the *Prince* was before it was a privateer, when we were children?"

"Yes."

"Didn't you ever ponder that if Mama had gone with Father on a voyage or two, their marriage would have been better?"

"I don't know. Their marriage was good until the war came."

"Well, I'm going. Wherever Nate asks me to."

I fell silent, thinking of Louis.

"Oh, Hannah, I'm sorry." She hugged me. "I shouldn't have said such to you. I'm being dim-witted and not sensible of your feelings."

"No, no, it's all right." I smiled at her. "I made my decision and it shouldn't affect your happiness. If it was right for me, I would have done it."

"You'll find someone, Hannah." Her eyes twinkled. "And don't forget, there's always Richard."

I blushed. "I'm not even looking," I confided. "Least of all at Richard." I smiled at her. Why did I suspect she didn't believe me? Then I minded how all of us in the family had been affected by our parents' disastrous marriage. "I am happy for you, Abby. And I shall miss you."

"And I, you. But you'll come to visit at Nate's father's plantation when we get home? Promise?"

I promised and we hugged again. "We must get down to breakfast or Father will become suspicious. Get dressed, quickly. I think he's brought guests. And do take down those drawers."

"You should take a swatch of material from them and put them in the quilt, Hannah. They were my signal flag."

"Abby! You scandalize me!"

"Nobody would have to know, except us." She giggled.

I would miss that giggle, I minded, going downstairs. How would I ever live without her?

Chapter Five

Our two breakfast guests were Mr. Leonard and Mr. Somers, the men I'd given the party for in January.

"You remember my daughters?" my father said as Abby and I went into the dining room.

They both stood and bowed. "How can we forget the lovely party Miss Hannah hosted for us?" Mr. Somers asked.

"How could we forget the lovely Miss Hannah herself?" asked Leonard.

I did not like Leonard. There was about him the essence of a weasel. And he had flirted shamelessly with me in January. Now he leaped forward to pull out my chair. Everyone sat. I saw the beleaguered look on Lawrence's face. I knew he hated these two men and the whole idea of the cotton yarn manufactory they were starting with father's partnership and money.

Dear God, I prayed silently, don't let him start talking about things like disease and corruption now. Even though he's right about the mill bringing such.

And also, God, I prayed, while You are listening, please help Mattie and Margaret to handle these unexpected guests. And don't let Thankful say anything to Father about Abby's elopement. And please don't let Father notice the lump on Cabot's forehead.

Oh, how could I ever hold everything together?

Then Mattie and Margaret brought the steaming silver platters of eggs, fresh fish, father's vegetables, warm biscuits, and ham, the silver urns of tea and coffee. I caught Margaret's eye over my father's head as she served him some vegetables and fish. And her look becalmed me.

"What brings you gentlemen to Salem?" I asked.

"Would you consider me bold if I said it was to see you, Miss Hannah?" Leonard asked.

"Yes."

He looked properly chastised. "Your father leaves in a week. We came to give him reports on our progress."

"And what progress have you made since January?" I did not care. But it was my duty as hostess to keep the flow of conversation going.

"We're building a three-story brick building on the five acres we purchased in North Beverly," Leonard said smugly. "By October we hope to have the first cotton yarn manufactory in America in operation."

I saw Lawrence scowl.

Leonard saw it, too. "We have a twofold purpose," he said in that smooth voice of his. "First we wish to make a profit. Second, we want to help Americans grow less dependent on English textiles."

"And don't forget," Somers added, "we'll be providing jobs for women who would otherwise be on public assistance. We know how many widows there are from the recent war. And we feel the obligation to help them make their way."

Poppycock, I thought. But I did not say it.

Lawrence did. In his own Lawrence-like way. "What kind of jobs?" he demanded. "Like those in the English factory system?"

"Lawrence, we've been through this before," my father said wearily. "I promised you that this cotton factory will never repeat the mistakes made in England."

I saw Lawrence's shoulders slump. Father knew just how to take the wind out of his sails, by speaking to him with bored indifference.

"We will provide for the health and virtue of our women workers," Father said.

"And do you think they need their virtue provided?" Lawrence asked.

Father flushed. "Women are the spinners and weavers in the home," he went on. "And English imports are eroding the American household industry. It is this I hope to remedy, Lawrence. We hope to have women weave cloth in their homes, from our yarns."

Leonard smiled at each of us, then. "I see the employment of women as an honorable stage in a young girl's life, allowing her to help her family or earn dowry money she may not otherwise have," he said.

Everyone was silent. Lawrence looked about to retort, but I kicked him under the table.

"There's a ship launching today," I said suddenly.

"Yes, there is." Father smiled at his guests. "Perhaps you gentlemen would like to walk to my counting house and watch. We'll have refreshments. All of Salem turns out for a ship launching. Church bells toll, schools are let out, there's music, cheer, and parties."

"May I go with you, Father?" Thankful asked.

"Of course, of course."

Cabot said nothing. The invitation did not include him and he knew it. As I knew, he would go on his own, haunting his favorite places on the wharves.

"Father, I must speak with you this morning," I said.

He looked across the long table at me. Both the blue eye and the green one managed equal frostiness. His narrow face, made shrewd by years of privateering, now appeared to me like that of a fox. His red hair touched with gray added to the illusion. "I always have time for my family," he said. "But I wish you to do something for me, first, Hannah."

I waited.

"Our guests are experienced in the makings and finishings of corduroys, quiltings, dimities, and God knows what else in England. Of course, you know England has a flourishing textile industry and guards her secrets for producing textiles well. Our guests are willing to lend us their expertise. And have a curiosity about your quilt. I would have you show it to them this morning after breakfast."

My hand flew to my throat. Dear God, didn't I have enough on my mind this day? Was Father pushing Leonard at me?

"Of course," I said. "If Abby and Thankful are agreeable. It's their quilt, too."

"Certainly." Abby smiled brightly. "As long as they don't take me prisoner to work in their cotton manufactory."

Was I the only one to hear her emphasis on the word *prisoner*?

After the meal was over, I touched Lawrence's shoulder as I passed his chair.

"An honorable stage in a woman's maturity," he whispered. "What a rotter that Leonard is. If he says one unseemly thing to you, Hannah, I'll challenge him to a duel."

"He's a fool, Lawrence. I can always handle a fool. Come see me later. I have something wonderful to tell you."

As I followed the others into the hall, I heard Father whisper to Abby, "Don't be sassy, miss.

Or I just might put you to work in the cotton manufactory."

It was said in jest. But there was a bit of urgency in the whisper and a hint of threat that sent a shiver down my spine.

Our quilting frame, made for us by Lawrence, was set up in the back parlor on four Windsor chairs.

"The border is already done," I explained to our guests. "We are presently cutting the individual patches that will be sewn together to form the blocks, then set into the quilt backing."

"And what name have you given the quilt?" Mr. Leonard asked. "All quilts have names, don't they? Like ships?"

"Trust," I said.

"An odd name for a quilt."

"Not at all. Is not trust the one commodity that is dearest in all our transactions?"

His eyes went over me in a way that was most unsettling. So, I had not been wrong. This man was wicked.

"How much wadding are you using?" he asked.

"One-half pound to the square yard."

"And your color scheme?"

"Different for everyone who has a place in the quilt. We will accept color as offered to us by the person asked to be part of it."

"Isn't that rather haphazard planning?" he persisted.

"Life is haphazard, or so I have learned, Mr. Leonard."

He smiled. "Fabric?"

"Again, whatever is offered. My father's old shirt from war days, for instance. It's homespun. So is the material from Mattie's skirt."

He raised his eyebrows. "Mattie is your serving girl, is she not?"

My face flamed. "She works for us. But she is a trusted friend."

"Ah, then one does not have to be a member of the family to be part of the quilt?"

"No."

"Only trusted?"

I felt myself snared. Like an animal in a trap. "Yes."

"Then perhaps someday," and he bowed, "I will have a place in the quilt, too."

"The place must be earned, Mr. Leonard."

He nodded. "I would make you a proposition, Miss Hannah. You are just the kind of person we need to instruct our women workers in the diverse points of the trade. Would you consider teaching our home weavers appreciation of fabric?"

He looked at my father, not me, as he said this. My father inclined his head in approval.

"I think not," I said quickly. "With Father gone, I'll have all I can do to keep his hearth and home in order."

"You could visit them in their homes at your leisure," Leonard insisted.

"It is something to consider, Hannah," my father said. "I have considerable investment in the cotton manufactory."

"I think not," I said again. I was very strong, saying it. But my heart was hammering inside me. The man wanted a chance to have more to do with me. I would not give it to him.

"Well, perhaps you'll have a change of heart," Father suggested.

Mr. Leonard's eyes then fell on the blue coat Thankful had brought down from the attic. "Speaking of fabric from the war," he said, crossing the room and picking up the coat. "This is as fine a specimen as I have ever seen."

"Of what?" I asked.

Leonard held the coat in his hands and looked at me as if I were suddenly dim-witted. "I thought you knew your fabric, Miss Hannah. This is a British officer's coat. I recognize the fine texture of the wool." He held it up. "Superb craftsmanship." He turned to my father, then.

"It's a British naval officer's coat. Wherever did you get it?"

Chapter Six

I closed the door to my father's study behind me and stood with my back braced against it, for support.

In his hand he held the blue coat.

"And I suppose this is a final act of sass to me, including this in your quilt."

It was like a continued conversation. As if there was only one conversation going on between us, the gist of which was that his children were working against him all the time.

He was a tall man, my father, but I noticed then that age seemed to be breathing on him, a hound catching up to the fox.

His tallness was becoming brittleness. He was becoming a dry wisp of a man. As if the fire of anger was devouring him from within. His hair, once a vibrant red, was streaked with gray. His skin was paling. He would one day disappear, I decided. Right in front of my eyes.

Could I wait that long to stop being afraid of him?

"I know nothing about the coat," I said quietly.

He grunted. "Where did it come from, then?"

"Thankful brought it down from the attic."

He threw the coat over a nearby chair. "It belonged to that British cur who came into this house when I was away! The one your mother befriended!"

Oh, I thought. And it took me a moment to absorb that fact. And oh, I thought again, I see what Thankful has done. How could I have been so blind?

"Mother did not defend the British officer," I said in a dead voice. "She had him and the others arrested."

"You *believe* this? Then why did she keep the coat?"

For that I had no answer.

"Believe it then, girl. I'll not take the belief away from you. Just tell me one thing. If you didn't know what the coat represents, why think to include it in the quilt?"

"It's blue. Mama's favorite color."

"I know what her favorite color was. I know everything there was to know about her. More than I'd like to."

There it was again, the whispered hint that he could tell me things about my mother that only he knew. Things he was keeping from me for my own good. My mind was so befuddled, I couldn't think for a moment.

"Couldn't you have taken some other piece of blue fabric from your mother's things?" he asked.

"I could not, Father. Thankful said you threw out all Mother's things."

He scowled. "They were ruined in the move here in the rain, which is why I disposed of them. You think I *threw them out* because they were your mother's?"

"I know only what Thankful told me."

His eyes narrowed when I spoke of Thankful. His favorite, his darling. Some color came into his face. "The child has a fanciful imagination. Of course, fanciful or not, she couldn't know about this coat."

I said nothing.

"Could she?" And he lifted his gaze to me.

"I think she knows," I said. "And I think that's why she gave it to me to bring here this morning. To make mischief. It is her favorite occupation."

"These are serious charges you bring against your sister."

I raised my chin and met his gaze. "She listens behind doors, pokes her nose where it doesn't belong, and reads other people's mail. She makes it her business to know about matters that will cause trouble. Have you ever spoken about that British officer when she might have been listening?"

He scowled, saying nothing. Then he reddened.

"You told her about the British officer Mama once fed?" I asked.

He nodded. "She's a bright child. She heard stories about it. I told her, yes. She's a restless, bright child. She should have been a boy."

He *would* make such excuses for her. "Which brings us to what I would ask you then, Father. She wants to go to Ohio with you. I think you should take her."

The eyes, both green and blue, grew darker, as they did when he was confronting a thought for the first time.

"I can no longer make her mind. If you leave her here, I can no longer be responsible for her. She is very bright, very quick. Ofttimes, she outwits me, as with this business of the coat. I have taken her as far as I can, Father. It is your turn now."

He paced the Persian carpet in front of his desk. I becalmed myself. I had him thinking.

"She knows she is special to you," I went on. "And because of this she knows she holds sway over all of us. Even Lawrence. This is not good for anyone in the family. And she runs wild outside the house. I don't know where she is half the time."

I knew he could not resist that argument. Ornery as he was to us, his own children, inside the house, I knew that above all he wanted to maintain the appearance of a solid family in town. That was important to him.

"How did the child know whose coat this was?" he mused to himself.

"She is a child no longer," I said. "That is how. She makes it her business to know such things."

That thought gave him pause. He seemed less sure of himself as he faced me across the Persian carpet. "Then you have not done a very good job with her upbringing."

I felt rage in my breast. How like him to blame me! But I kept calm. "Certainly it is incumbent upon you to take her then, if I have so failed," I said.

He nodded. "Send her to me," he directed.

It was done! He would take her! I turned to leave, but he stopped me. "Hannah."

I turned.

He was holding the blue coat. He came forward and thrust it into my hand. "I want this burned. Do you hear?"

"Yes, sir."

"Must I instruct Margaret to do it?"

"I will do it, Father."

"And one more thing. Mr. Leonard will give you a piece of fabric. He will be in the quilt."

My mouth fell open. I felt the breath go out of me, as if I'd been slapped. "By what right?"

"I have backed him and Somers, financially. There is trust between us. We expect to produce eight thousand yards of cloth from our cotton yarn by the end of next year. His piece will be from the first yard to come off the looms."

I felt sick. "I will not have that man a part of my quilt!"

"Do as I say, Hannah." He sounded bored, as he did when he spoke to Lawrence. "He will send the fabric to you. Or perhaps bring it to you himself."

"I'll not receive him. Can't you see how he leers at me?"

"Stop being a child, Hannah. The man is of substance and purpose. A far better prospect than your Louis."

I whirled on him. "Leave Louis out of this!"

He smiled. He could smile with more cruelty than any man I had ever known. "I'm sorry, Hannah, for not being so sensible of your feelings." His voice was as smooth as silk. "All I'm saying is you'd do well to be more amiable to him when he comes to call in the future."

"I'll *not* receive him."

"You will," he said. "Send Thankful to me. And see that her things are packed in time."

Chapter Seven

When everyone left the house that morning, I left, too. I had to leave, get out, walk, or I would go mad. So I changed into my warmest woolen petticoat and short gown, put on my sturdiest shoes and cloak, and began to walk.

I was not surprised to find myself going in the direction of the wharves. Half the town was going to Becket's Shipyard to see the launching.

I was going to see the *Swamp Fox*. To visit Nate Videau. This was as good a time as any. I needed to speak with someone who was not part of Salem town and its doings, someone who stood outside my family yet could probably tell me more about it than anyone.

But I was going for another reason, too.

I had just traded off one sister for the other. I had just convinced Father to take Thankful to Ohio with him, as she'd demanded. And I'd done it so Thankful wouldn't tell him about Abby's elopement.

I had met Nate before, of course, conversed with

him and liked him. But I wanted to satisfy myself once again before they left.

"How nice to see you, Miz Hannah. What kin ah do for y'all?"

I looked up into the black face of the man at the top of the gangway. This would be Merlin, according to Abby. "I wish to see your master. Is he aboard?"

"He be in the captain's cabin. You jus' follow me. Watch your step there. Right this way."

The deck of the *Swamp Fox* was deserted, nevertheless I kept my eyes down as I followed the man. We crossed the scrubbed quarterdeck and went down the steps of the companionway. Below deck I stopped and looked around.

I had not been on a ship in years, not even one of our father's, but it was all familiar to me. Abby had been right. This was as good as the *Prince* in her prime, a true marriage of strength and beauty. I saw gleaming brass whale oil lamps, shining small square windows, solid sea chests, canvas bags, carved doors that led to cabins. And, built into the gunports, the cannon Abby had spoken of.

I stood for a moment breathing in the familiar smells and sensations from my childhood. I heard water lapping gently at the ship's sides. The noise of the crowd passing by on the way to the launching receded. I felt safe and secure here.

Merlin was knocking on an ornate door.

"Enter."

"There be a lady here to see you, suh. Miz Hannah."

"Miz Hannah! What a surprise. Do come in. Merlin, we'll have tea. And cakes. Y'all have been baking, I can smell it."

"Yessuh. Fresh cornbread."

"Good. Have Liddy bring some with the tea."

Merlin left. Nate Videau kissed my hand, helped remove my cloak, and moved some books off an upholstered chair. "Ah never can come into any port without buying more books. They're my weakness." He placed the volumes next to some others on built-in shelves behind him.

I stared. There had to be three dozen books on those shelves, some morocco-bound. Midway between arranging them, he turned.

"Is something wrong at home? Is Abby all right?"

I took some folded and sealed vellum out of my reticule. "Abby's fine. Sends you this. Go ahead and read it, while I look around."

The cabin was both elegant and cosy, the mid-morning light muted by shutters. On the cherry desk were partially unrolled maps, books, a carved ivory chess set, and a crystal decanter with two clean glasses. A comfortable chair was beneath the windows. In the corner was a globe of the world. On the bottom bookshelf behind him was an open case, velvet-lined.

Inside were two dueling pistols.

Also on one of those shelves was a sheathed

sword. His jacket lay over a chair. He wore a spotless shirt, black stock at the neck, ruffles at the cuffs. I smelled tobacco, saw pipes in a rack. And then the bird.

It was eyeing me from within a brass cage in a corner.

"Ohhh, a parrot!" I got up. "I love parrots. May I?"

"Certainly. His name is Cornwallis. But don't go poking your finger in the cage. Your little brother does that all the time."

"Cabot? He's been here?"

"Many times, Miz Hannah. Ah've been teaching him about the sea. Right smart boy he is, too."

I sighed. "I wish he was as interested in his lessons."

"He considers ships and the sea his lessons."

I turned to face Nate Videau. He had put Abby's note aside and was studying me with eyes that were smiling, but wise. I smiled back at him.

"Do I pass muster, Miss Hannah? Ah know you haven't had enough time in the past to inspect me."

I blushed. But I liked his honesty. And so decided he deserved mine. "Yes, you do, Mr. Videau. I like what I see."

"Ah'm gratified. Yours is the second visit ah've had this week from a Chelmsford."

"You mean Cabot."

"No, that would make it three. Your brother Lawrence stopped by yesterday. Thought it only right, since ah'll be marrying his sister. If y'all are here to make sure ah'll take care of Abby, why rest your mind. Lawrence already assured himself of that."

I smiled. "My visit has even a deeper meaning, Mr. Videau."

"Do sit, please. And call me Nate. We'll be kin soon. And tell me about your deeper meaning."

So I told him. About how I'd traded off one sister for the other. I told him about Thankful threatening to tell about the elopement, everything.

"Ah see." He nodded, contemplating. "And so you came to make sure y'all did the right thing?"

"How can any of it be right, Nate? I feel guilty already about sending Thankful off to the wilderness." I spoke with a passion I seldom let strangers see. "She's a troublesome little piece. She plagues me no end. But she's still my sister. And I do love her. Did I have the right to do what I did?"

"Seems to me it was she who wanted it," he said softly.

"I'll still always blame myself if something goes wrong."

He nodded. "You've taken too much on yourself, Hannah. We can do only so much for others. But we mustn't allow them to eat us alive."

I sat. The sound of his voice, with its honeyed tones, lulled me. He seemed so confident, so sure. Just being in his presence soothed me.

Then a petite nigra woman came in with a tray

of tea and cakes. He introduced her. "This is Liddy. She'll be your sister's personal maidservant."

The woman curtsied. "I'll be her companion when she needs one, too," she said.

Such perfect diction. I watched her pour the tea. She had a natural grace about her.

"I hope Lawrence minded his manners when he was here," I told Nate. "He can be surly at times."

"Lawrence?" He laughed. "We had supper and traded war stories over a bottle of my best Madeira. He helped put down Shay's Rebellion."

"And you were in the war."

"Yes." He sobered, remembering. "Ah fought with Francis Marion. My sister gave him aid. He was our cousin. Many times she brought information to him from behind enemy lines, to his hideouts. Ah was just sixteen. He was my hero. My father made me wait until ah was sixteen to join him. That wasn't until 1780."

He balanced his teacup. So, he was twenty-four. Big hands, but not ungainly. He went silent then and would talk no more of the war, or what he'd done with Francis Marion at age sixteen. He smiled at me. I smiled back. Something about him, I decided. What?

Someone had cared for him well in his youth, given him confidence. He moved his large frame with grace. No, something else there was. What?

A quiet strength, I saw, deftly contained under a gentleness he'd honed to perfection. Oh, I envied Abby. He would be strong for her, yet gentle enough to understand why she needed his strength.

"So, Lawrence is giving the bride away," he told me.

"Yes," I said.

"He's also helping Abby out of the house that night. He intends to get stone drunk."

"But Lawrence never imbibes too much."

"Exactly. Ah'll be waiting for them both outside. My carriage will be down the street."

"How will Abby get away from the party?"

"Ah understand your father does not condone impertinence?"

"You understand correctly."

"She intends to be impertinent to him in front of the guests when he berates Lawrence for drinking."

"Then Father will send her upstairs."

"Yes. In case y'all are wondering, Hannah, ah don't aim to stay at sea my whole life. Ah'll be settling down soon to run my father's plantation, which will one day be mine."

"You're a good man. I am envious of Abby. Oh, I must tell you. My friend, Mary Lander, is going to stand up for Abby at the wedding."

He nodded. "Richard's mother. He's my best man."

"So I heard."

Our eyes met. He set his cup down and smiled. "Ah've heard how you turned down an offer of marriage to please your father. May ah be impertinent enough to say that ah hope you don't make a habit of doing that?"

"I don't have any other offers to turn down, Nate."

"That's not what Cabot says."

"Cabot!" I sighed. "I suppose he's talking about Richard Lander."

"Lander's a good man. And right fond of y'all."

I bit down a saucy reply. This man was genuinely concerned about me. He did not deserve sauciness. Then a thought came to me. "Tell me, Nate, do you think Lander is outfitting the *Prince* for the slave trade?"

He considered the question. "No. Seems to me there's a secrecy about the voyage, yes. But ah don't think it has to do with running West Indies sugar and molasses here to make Yankee rum to take to West Africa's gold coast and pick up African slaves to take to West Indies sugar plantations. But if he was, would it matter to you?"

"Yes, Nate. We don't take kindly to slave traders here in Salem."

"Ah know that. But what will your daddy's cotton mill do to those who work in it? The people in the English mills are worse off than our nigras, ah can vouch for that."

"Your point is well taken, Nate. But I couldn't consider a future with Richard Lander if he were running a slaver."

He nodded. "Lander has a passion about keeping

this voyage a secret," he said. "You know him. Would he care what people said about him if he fancied being captain of a slaver?"

I was thunderstruck. "No, he wouldn't."

"Then ah speculate the secrecy is for something far different."

My spirits lifted. "Thank you, Nate. You've helped me much."

"Ah wish there was more ah could do for you, Hannah."

"You're doing it," I said, "by marrying Abby."

He showed me about the ship, then, explaining that his crew was in town. And it was all just as Abby had described it. When I left, he kissed my hand again. "If there's ever anything ah can do for y'all, Hannah, write to my father's plantation."

He pressed a piece of paper into my hand. On it was the address. Then he kissed me again. On the forehead. "We're kin," he said.

I truly felt it when I left. And I was glad I'd come. I went home feeling less guilty over trading off Thankful for Abby and sure I'd done the right thing, after all.

Chapter Eight

I did not like Mrs. Haffield White. She was one of those women who was always right as rain about everything.

I did not like people who were right all the time. Only God had such a privilege. But in Salem town, God shared it with Mrs. Haffield White. And, like most people who know they are right about things, she talked all the time.

I had to invite her to the party because I'd asked the wives and families of the men in Salem who had left on the first two trips west. And Mrs. White's husband and two sons, Josiah and Peletiah, had left in early December.

Father had wanted me to invite only the financial backers of the expedition. Halfway through the party, I wished I had listened to him. I wished, too, that Parson Bentley had been able to come. He was a dear friend as well as our pastor at East Church. But he was out of town.

Dinner was over. Margaret and Mattie and the extra girls hired were clearing the table in preparation for bringing in the tea and cake. My father had taken the men to his library for cigars and rum and to talk business. The children were playing upstairs. The women had taken chairs in front of the fireplace and were knitting caps and warm hose for their relatives out west, to be delivered by Father's expedition.

"I hear you're sending your sister Thankful along," Mrs. White said. Her knitting needles clicked as she said it.

Everyone looked up at her, then at me.

"Yes," I said, "she's begged to go. And Father's agreed to take her."

"They'll only have temporary shelter when they get there, you know," Mrs. White said. "My Haffield writes that they are still clearing land and laying out the town. I don't know as I'd send a young girl like that out. Just yet."

"Father says it's safe," I countered.

"What do you consider safe, Hannah?" Mrs. White asked. She was knitting faster than ever.

"The fort they're building," I answered. "*Campus Martius.*"

"And why do you suppose they are *building* the fort, Hannah?" she persisted.

I did not answer. Wordlessly, I glanced at the other women in the group. Mrs. Ezekiel Cooper met my eyes briefly and looked down at her own handiwork. Elderly Mrs. William Moulton would not look at me at all.

The word hung in the air between us. *Indians.*

Nobody connected with the migrations to Ohio would speak of the threat of Indians. It was just not done. But now I saw that they were on the minds of all the ladies present.

I felt dizzy and sick inside. *They blame me, because I'm sending my sister west,* I thought. If something happens to her, they won't blame Father, they'll blame me.

Never mind who was blamed. *Suppose something happened to Thankful?* It didn't even have to be Indians. It could be anything. Oh, dear God, I thought, what have I done?

"Excuse me," I said getting up. "I have to see to the cake."

In the kitchen I bumped into Lawrence. He'd just come in the back door.

"What's wrong, Hannah? You look as if you need a brace of cold air."

I looked up at my handsome older brother. "The women think it's awful that I'm sending Thankful on the trip."

"Those old hens? They're jealous of you, Hannah. Because you're young and hostess in this grand house. Those old codfish aristocrats can't accept that. They don't accept Father, but for his money. Even though they look down on it because it's new. Besides, you aren't sending Thankful, Father is."

"They blame me, Lawrence. And so do I. Suppose something happens to her? Father would never have agreed if I hadn't pushed for it."

"Something happen to Thankful?" He laughed.

"Yes, suppose she gets bitten by a snake or . . ." My voice faltered.

"Say it, Hannah. It'll make you feel better. Attacked by an Indian."

I looked at him. "The *Salem Mercury* reports that the Indians are not happy with the influx of people."

"And the snakes? What does the *Mercury* say of them?"

"Oh, Lawrence, be serious."

"I am. And I'd say the snakes and Indians should be warned that Thankful is coming."

I hugged him. "I'll miss you so. You always could make things look right."

"Forget Thankful for a minute and come outside and see the sign I've painted for the wagon."

The March evening was unusually warm. The wagon, set behind our house, looked like an ark. I took comfort from its great bulk and strength. It was covered with black canvas. On each side Lawrence had painted, in lovely large white letters, *For the Ohio at the Muskingum.*

Muskingum. An Indian name for a river and a valley.

"It's lovely, Lawrence," I said.

"I feel so different about this expedition, since you and Mattie came up with the idea of my painting the Indians," he said.

"It was Mattie's idea, Lawrence."

"Yes. She's a dear girl." But he would say no more. And I did not push him.

"Will you be up when we leave at first light tomorrow?" he asked.

"I wouldn't miss it."

"Don't worry about Thankful. The trip will do the little chit good. I'll keep an eye out for her. Now tell me, shall I wait until after the cake to go into my act and insult Leonard?"

"Not Leonard, please, Lawrence."

"Yes. It's my chance. Don't deny me, Hannah."

"Just don't call him out for a duel. Promise."

"If you will promise me that you'll let Cabot show you how to fire a pistol. Just in case Leonard makes a nusiance of himself."

"I don't need to learn how to fire a pistol."

"But I need your promise."

I smiled and said I would. "But I thought you commissioned Cabot to be man of the house and look after me."

"I had to. The poor little fellow has dug himself a hole and is ready to climb into it since he found out Thankful is going with us. Damn Father for what he's doing to that boy! I can take what he hands out, but Cabot can't. Why, Hannah, why does he dislike the little fellow so?"

I had thought the same but never said the words. Hearing them from Lawrence made them take on a life of their own. "I don't know," I said.

"It's better he isn't coming with us. Father would belittle him at every turn. You must work with him while we're gone, Hannah. Repair the damage Father has done."

"I will. I don't know how yet, but I'll find a way."

We walked back to the house. "Father doesn't know it yet, but I've been made second-in-command to Major John Burnham on this trip," he said quietly.

I stopped short and turned. "Oh, Lawrence, I'm so proud." Again I hugged him. "It's because of your militia experience!"

"Yes." He scowled. "But can Father defer to his own son? He's accustomed to command."

"Well, he'll have to become unaccustomed to it then. It's an honor and you deserve it."

He was pleased, I could see. And I was happy for him. Lawrence badly needed someone to recognize his abilities. And no wonder Burnham had put his trust in him. Lawrence had proved himself handsomely in Shay's. I'd seen him when he'd returned, in his rough militiaman's uniform, carrying knives and powder horn, ax and musket, wearing skins.

My hand had gone to my throat, seeing him.

He'd reminded me of Louis. I'd seen that same touch of fearlessness about him that Louis had learned on the frontier.

"It is the Shawnee warriors I'd like to meet and paint," he said. "I've heard they're the finest specimens of Indians in the land."

"Louis wrote me of them," I said.

"Did Louis meet any of them?"

"Yes."

He looked down at me. "Do you still love Louis, Hannah?"

The question was so soft it was like an echo of my own thoughts. "I don't know, Lawrence. I think of him often. I've grieved him, I know that. And I feel guilty because of it. If I had loved him enough, I would have gone with him, wouldn't I have?"

"Things aren't that simple," he said. "Would to God they were. Does he still write to you?"

"No."

"What if he comes back?"

I hadn't thought of that. "Do people come back from the west?"

"I certainly intend to."

What if he comes back? I felt a chill, like someone was walking over my grave. Then I shook it off. "He loves it out there. It's all he ever talked about. Settling." I smiled. "Anyway, I've more than that to think on. Richard Lander's asked me to wait for him."

"Good!" He sighed and looked up at the great shadow of the house looming over us. "What did you say to that?"

"Nothing, yet."

"Well, I feel better leaving here knowing that. You'll have a fight on your hands with Father."

"Would that be anything new, Lawrence?"

He laughed. "Not as much of a fight as I'll have

when he finds out about me and Mattie." He looked at the ground. "Mayhap it's best I'm leaving. Before I do wrong by the girl."

I was touched by this. It was the first he'd spoken of Mattie to me. "We all need time," I told him. "And I'll look after her for you."

We went into the house then, sharing a new closeness. No more words were needed between us. It was, he said, time to do his performance.

Lawrence performed well. There was, I saw, a touch of the artist about him. He'd visited London with Father at sixteen and gone to many plays at Covent Garden Theatre. And I minded how they'd fired him up. But this performance had an air of something more than theater about it.

It had an air of rebellion against Father. For how he'd treated Abby. And it came to me, as I watched, that Lawrence was putting his heart and soul into buying Abby her freedom.

There was a toast first, as everyone stood around the dining room table. The cake was cut. Father gave a speech. He was in full mettle, in charge. I saw a glance exchanged between Lawrence and Abby across the table, then Lawrence went into his act.

The toasts were many. To my father, to Rufus Putnam and Reverend Manesseh Cutler, directors of the Ohio Company. To the first two groups already gone west.

Then Lawrence proposed a toast. Wavering on

his feet, looking sufficiently glassy-eyed, he raised his goblet.

"To Mr. Leonard, whose lofty goal is to introduce the English factory system to America, to provide for the virtue of our wives, daughters, and sisters."

The room went dead quiet. Lawrence continued. "There are some who say he will also introduce us to the misery and poverty that is the lot of English mill workers. But then, Mr. Leonard has assured us that a factory town need not be a symbol of vice and poverty. Haven't you, Mr. Leonard?"

"Lawrence, you're drunk," Father said disgustedly.

"Am I, Father?" Lawrence smiled. "But drunks and fools say the truth, don't they?"

"You may admit to being both, but that doesn't excuse you," Father said. "Apologize to Mr. Leonard."

All eyes were on Lawrence. Then Abby came around the table to stand by her brother. She leaned against his arm.

"I'll take him upstairs, Father."

"You'll do nothing of the kind until he apologizes."

Several of the guests had wandered away from the table, but were still within earshot.

"He doesn't mean it, Father," Abby said.

"Ah, but I do," Lawrence insisted. Then he burped, most ungraciously. Several of the women gasped. I almost smiled.

"Do mean it." Lawrence put his arm around his sister. "And you all remember someday, when that cotton manufactory is thumping away, that right here in this house Lawrence Chelmsford warned you about the evil of it. And that man there," he pointed at Father, "threatened Abby that she'd work in the factory if she didn't mind him. Didn't he, Abby?"

Abby took up the cue. "Yes, he did," she said. "Of course, Lawrence, it might be better than what I have now. Being kept a prisoner in my own room. You didn't know that, did you?" Her voice was clear and loud and firm.

Everyone listened.

"My father keeps me prisoner in my room. Night and day. Because my beau has dropped anchor in harbor!"

I knew, at once, what Abby was doing. And in my heart I cheered her on. We all were sensible of the fact that everyone outside our home saw our father as a pillar of Salem society, a hero of the Revolution, a model parent.

Everyone held him in high esteem. Except his own children. Not even Thankful liked him. But she had learned how to use him.

Now Abby saw her chance to tell them what kind of man our father was. Well, everyone was paying her mind, all right. Because Abby had always been much loved by our neighbors and friends.

I realized, as I searched out their faces, that this

was her goodbye to them. That she was determined to let them know what she'd been through. So when they spoke of her and Nate afterwards, when they clucked their wagging tongues over the elopement, it might be with a degree of understanding and sympathy.

Because Abby wanted to be able to come back to Salem someday with Nate. Good for you, Abby, I thought.

"Out of my sight, both of you!"

Oh, we could always count on Father, couldn't we?

Fear-quickened, I walked across the room to Lawrence and Abby. Father's face had gone from red to white, then red again. He looked as if he might go into apoplexy.

"I'll take them upstairs, Father," I said. "Come along, you two. For shame. Please, everyone, accept my apologies. My brother Lawrence never could hold his liquor."

So, it was over then. Done with. Lines drawn in our house as on a battlefield. Lines that could never be crossed back over again.

Well, I minded, climbing the stairs, it's been coming for a long time. It isn't anything that started here tonight.

Up in Abby's room, I hugged both her and Lawrence. I held my sister's slender form close to me. "You were wonderful, both of you."

"We're not safe yet." Lawrence got busy.

Quickly he positioned himself on the roof outside the widow's walk, to attach Abby's last portmanteau to the rope and lower it down.

"We're right on time, you two, hurry up," he whispered.

I helped Abby change out of her party dress and into her sturdier travel clothes. "Trousers!" I gasped as I watched her slip into a pair that had once belonged to Lawrence.

"You wouldn't have me climb down that ladder in skirts, would you?" She giggled. "Not that it'd bother me. But if I look like a man, running for the carriage, it'll be better all around."

Dressed, and with her curls tucked under one of Lawrence's hats, she faced me.

And it was time for goodbye.

I didn't know how to say goodbye. Words were stupid. They said so little. Yet they opened up holes you could fall into and never climb out of again.

"Oh, Abby, I wish I could be there! I wish I could stand by you when you say the words and become married."

"You will be," she said.

Abby knew what words to say. Her words were sparse, but somehow they covered the situation. And yes, she was right. I would be there in spirit.

"I'll write to you, Hannah. Oh, I hope he doesn't blame you for this."

"I can take the blame. As long as I know you're happy."

She hugged me. "I'm going to be happier than anybody ever was, Hannah. I promise you that."

Again, she was saying what I needed to hear. Telling me the price was worth it. Sending Thankful off, defying Father. *You've done right, Hannah, she was saying. Don't fear.*

There was time for no more. We hugged again and I helped her out the window to the roof where Lawrence had brought the rope ladder up again.

He brought Nate with it. Nate, his large, graceful frame between us and the dark unknown. As it should be, I minded. As it should be. "Go on, Lawrence," he said.

Lawrence went down. We heard him hit the ground. Nate turned to me. "Ah'd admire for y'all to write to us," he said.

I promised.

Then Nate hugged me. "Ah'm gratified for what y'all have done. Y'all made this possible. And ah won't forget it."

I mumbled something about it being worth every minute of it. "Go," I said. "Now, quickly."

One more y'all and I'd start bawling like a stuck pig.

Nate pulled up the rope ladder and Abby hugged him around the back and unself-consciously wrapped her legs around him. Under one arm she had her portion of the quilt, which I'd cut off for her that morning.

Goodbye, they both murmured.

Goodbye.

And so they went. And so I stood alone on the roof, my skirts billowing in the night breezes. I waited until they got to the ground, watched them bound across the grass, grateful for the darkness. At the edge of our property they turned and waved and ran off into the night.

The worst thing I had to do in my life was go back into Abby's room and see her party dress and petticoats on the floor. The room where she'd done all her girlish planning and dreaming, where she'd hung her lacy drawers on the roof to send signals to Nate. I looked around me. All her things were gone.

But the room was haunted already. I could smell the fragrance of the soap she used to wash her hair. The bed, the chair, the bookshelves mocked me.

I went back down to our guests.

Abby gone. My mind was with them all night. Now their chaise has reached the wharf. Now they're aboard. Now Reverend Cutler is there. Bless him. He'd made some excuse why he couldn't be at the party tonight, although he was one of the directors of the Ohio Company.

And Mary Lander, Mama's friend was there. And Richard. Now the reverend is saying the words over them.

Thankful came up to me as I was making small talk with Mrs. Shaw. "Well, did all go smoothly tonight?" Thankful asked.

"How did you know about the officer's coat?"

She smiled. "I asked Lawrence what it was. He told me. Of course, he didn't know *whose* it was. He's such an innocent. But I knew. It belonged to the man Mama once fed, who caused all the trouble."

I excused myself and pulled her into a corner. I gripped her arm. "Hear me now, Thankful Chelmsford, if you say *one* word to Father this night about what is going on, or one word after this night about who was involved and how, you will be doing the *filthiest* chores on your trip. Lawrence will see to it."

She smiled at me sweetly. "Lawrence never could make me mind. What makes you think he can start now? Especially after his performance tonight. He's fallen from grace with Father for good."

"Because." I measured out the words like bitter medicine. I forced them down her throat. "Because he has been made second-in-command to Major Burnham who leads this expedition. Which means he will have the authority to make you mind. And Father cannot protect you. Do you understand?"

She did. Her face went white. It may have been the only time in my life that I ever had the upper hand with my little sister. And I must say that I enjoyed it thoroughly.

Chapter Nine

"*Where is she? Hannah, come down this minute!*"

My father's voice bellowed through the house. It bounced off the windows. It made my head hurt.

I'd slept late and was struggling into my clothes. The house was wrapped in a gray mist. I tied my skirt, somehow did the hooks and eyes of my short gown, and stumbled into the hall.

Mattie was there, her face white, her blue eyes large. "Oh, Hannah, he's found out about Abby's elopement!"

I gripped her cold hand and started down. "Don't worry, Mattie, it will be all right."

It was a false promise, but it soothed her. For I knew it was not all right. I knew things would probably never be all right in our house again.

I went into the dining room, where the family was assembled. There sat Lawrence, Thankful, and Cabot. Lawrence's jaw was twitching, something that happened when things went bad. Thankful, dressed for her trip, had a half-smile on her face. Cabot had that look about him of wanting to melt into the wainscoting.

Father stood behind his chair at the head of the table. "Did you know about this?" he demanded as I entered the room. "A note came to the door this morning. Your sister has run off."

I hesitated. What profit in admitting it? But what virtue in the denial?

Lawrence must have been thinking in kind. "We all knew," he said. His voice was low, but it had a new timbre of authority. Lawrence, too, was dressed for his trip, in his militia clothing. "She loves him, Father," he said. "The girl has a right to be happy. You wouldn't grant it to her, so she took it on her own."

Second-in-command, I thought. Yes, he's deserving of it.

"What do you mean, you all knew?" Father demanded. He looked from one of us to the other.

"Just that," Lawrence said with dead finality. "It was plain to see what was going on with Abby, if you paid mind. The children had no part in it. But Hannah and I helped her. That's what I mean."

"How dare you?" Father looked from me to Lawrence, then back to me again, not knowing where to direct his wrath. His eyes came back to me. "So this is what you've been about. Plotting behind my back to help your sister run off with that Southern reprobate."

"He isn't a reprobate, Southern or any other

kind," Lawrence said wearily. "Stop it, Father. He's from a fine old family. They gave well in the war, almost everything they owned."

"So now he comes here to take what I own?"

"You didn't own Abby, Father. That's just it," Lawrence tried, dearly, to explain. "When will you learn? We're your children. But you don't own us and you can't be a dictator, like George III."

Father threw the note down on the floor. "I have people I can send to the wharves to bring her back if you won't go, Lawrence." He started out of the room. "How dare you compare me to the King I fought against?" There were tears in his eyes.

Lawrence's voice stopped him. "The *Swamp Fox* cleared Salem Harbor before midnight. They've gone, Father."

My father turned to look at Lawrence and it was as if he diminished in stature. He seemed shorter, frailer, less sure of himself with that news. The tears looked about to spill over.

Lawrence's jaw wasn't twitching anymore.

"She's married," he told Father. "They were wed last evening on the quarterdeck. I gave her away."

"Turncoat," my father hissed. "I'll not have you on this trip with me. I'll not have a turncoat by my side. Unpack your things!"

Lawrence sighed. "I've been made second-in-command, Father. It's too late for that now. It's too late for a lot of things. In heaven's name, this family is so broken. We're leaving on a trip. God knows when we'll be home again. Sit down and eat with us. Let's try, somehow, to salvage what we have left. In God's name, Father, sit."

Outside, an hour later, we stood together in the street in front of our house and watched as Lawrence directed the last-minute securing of barrels of salt water to the wagon. They were for Father's daily bathing.

I would be ever grateful to Lawrence for what he'd done in the dining room that morning. He'd taken charge. He'd gotten Father to sit down, asked me to say grace, and, as we ate, he'd told Father how Abby loved him in spite of what he'd done to her. He spoke to the children, admonishing Thankful that she must get along with others on the trip. He reminded Cabot that he would be the man of the house now, that we were all depending on him, and the boy actually smiled and sat taller in his chair.

He told us about Abby's wedding and relayed messages to each of us from her.

"We're a family," he said finally, "no matter where we go or what we do, we're bound to one another. That's what Abby wanted me to tell you all this morning."

Everyone listened. And if Father wasn't listening, at least he did not interrupt.

Second-in-command, I thought. Yes.

Then we went outside. Five other wagons were lined up behind ours, with patient oxen in the lead. So many families. At least six. I noted, with a sense of comfort, the placid strength on the faces of the women as everyone gathered so Reverend William Bentley could give a brief address, say a prayer, and wish them well.

I looked around me as the prayer was being said. Thankful was not paying mind. She was fussing with her woolen skirt. I caught her eye and scowled and she gave me a sassy look. Then Lawrence came up behind her and put a hand on her shoulder and she stood still and lowered her eyes.

It'll be all right, I told myself. But I was not ready for the leaving.

How could anybody be ready for that?

Major Burnham conferred with Lawrence, who immediately got the men in hand, gave the order, and three volleys of musket fire rang out in the street. The men threw their hats in the air, gave three huzzahs, and the women started toward their wagons with their families.

I went over to Thankful. In my hand was a bundle tied in cloth. Her part of the quilt. I gave it to her, hugged her. "Be good," I said. It was the wrong thing to say. She took the bundle, made a face, and danced away from me. "I'm going to have a wonderful time," she flung at me. Then she climbed up to the front seat of the wagon.

She looked so frail, sitting there. The hood of

her cloak fell back over her shoulders and her red hair stood out, so. It would make her a target, I thought grimly.

I had to stop thinking like that. There were other children in the group. I thought I counted several young boys and two young girls. But it was confusing. The mist was thick and people dipped in and out of it, were gone just as I caught sight of them.

Who were these families? I had invited them to the party, but they were too busy readying themselves for their trip and had declined. Why hadn't I taken the time to get to know the women before? I could have asked them to look out for my sister.

I looked up at Thankful again. She had a smile on her face, her eyes were bright. She was happy. Off on a fine adventure. And ready for it.

Why hadn't I known she was ready for it?

My mind went back, suddenly, to when Thankful was born. I was a child of three. Mother had said I would help care for her. I promised Mother I would. And I'd broken that promise.

There were things I should have told Thankful. Things about becoming a woman. I'd thought there was time. And now it had run out.

I'd planned a whole little speech for her this morning at this goodbye, a proper, older sister speech. And now, there she was, sitting in front of the wagon, next to Father. So high up, I couldn't reach her. And there was nothing I could say that she would listen to. Because she didn't need me.

I sighed and looked around. All up and down the street people were saying goodbye. I saw Lawrence standing to the side with Mattie. I saw him kiss her. Then a young boy came over, leading Lawrence's horse. He handed the reins to my brother and ran to his own wagon.

Lawrence hugged me. "Take care of yourself."

I looked up at him. Tried to imprint his face in my mind. Light hair, like Abby's, dark eyes. Mother's eyes. Strong chin and nose, cheekbones set already in the ways of a man. A good face. My heart was bursting with things to say. Memories and fears fought for places in my mind.

"Take care of yourself." It was stupid. But it was right at the same time.

"I will."

"Thank you for what you did at breakfast."

He nodded. "Look out for Cabot. And Mattie."

"I will."

"We'll try to write. The mails aren't good. If you don't get word on time don't worry."

"Yes."

He looked at Cabot. "You're in charge. I expect good things from you."

Cabot's chin trembled. "I should be going, Lawrence. I could be your adjunct instead of that other boy. I can fire a musket. You taught me."

"I don't want this now," Lawrence said. "There

isn't time for it. You're in charge here. You have to take care of things at home. He can't anymore." He jerked his head at Father. "So you and I have to. And now the job is yours."

Cabot nodded, accepting that. Lawrence patted his shoulder, then mounted his horse and took his place at the head of the caravan, beside Major Burnham.

"Father?" I looked up, craning my neck. "Aren't you going to say goodbye to us?" I stood there with my arm around Cabot.

He did not look. He did not answer. He stared straight ahead.

I felt slapped. "Father!" I demanded.

"I've nothing to say. Except that she's as bad as a doxie, running off like that. But what can I expect? She's her mother all over again."

It was spoken low and there was so much noise in the street, what with orders being shouted, people calling goodbyes, and dogs barking in excitement, that I was sure no one else had heard. I looked at Cabot. He hadn't heard, thank heaven.

Why did Father say Abby was Mother all over again?

The wagons were moving. "Thankful!" I called out.

It was in that moment that the scene froze before me, like a painting, and I had a revelation of sorts.

Thankful had become a woman, yes. She sat up there on that wagon seat and struck a fine figure of a woman, not a child. Certainly, in the past,

I'd noticed that her arms and chest were filling out. Now, even under the heavy clothing I saw it. She had grown up on her own, without my knowing it.

She smiled down at me.

I was frightened. My heart was bursting with things to say. I didn't know you'd traveled so far already, without me. I'm sorry, I wasn't part of those travels. Now, I won't be, either. I opened my mouth to speak. She was waiting.

"Don't forget to work on your piece of the quilt," I said.

She raised her eyes in mock despair. I stood with my arm around Cabot, feeling silly, watching the wagons move away. It was still misty and I could hear them as they melted into the mist.

So small, our wagon. Last night it had seemed so large and strong. What would it look like in the wilderness? I felt myself emptying out, hearing them clip-clopping away. My heart and soul, my blood and sinews seemed to be pulled out of me and going along with them. I stood there bereft and empty, with nothing left inside me at all.

Chapter Ten

July 1788

"Lost, lost, lost."

The voice of the town crier intoned the most dreadful words in Salem town. I looked across the room at Reverend Bentley as the crier passed under our parlor window.

He nodded at me and got up and crossed the room to shut the window against the sweet July air.

"Do they know the name of the lost ship yet?" I asked. It was the first time a ship had been lost since Nate and Abby had left.

"They think it's the *Cato*," he said. He sipped his tea. Between us, on the floor, was a sack of lemons. A ship had dropped anchor this day, its captain bringing not only the lemons but the news about the lost vessel.

"It could be the *Swamp Fox*." I had to say the words, for they lay between us like the sack of lemons. "She left on March fifteenth."

Reverend Bentley smiled weakly. "The *Cato* sailed on the twentieth," he reminded me.

"Then what would she be doing off the coast of Hispaniola in a hurricane?"

"What would the *Swamp Fox* be doing there, Hannah?"

"Lumber," I said. "Abby wrote me from Martinique at the end of April. Nate heard there'd been a terrible fire on Hispaniola and lumber was needed badly. Nate had much lumber in the hold. They set sail for Hispaniola soon after that."

"The *Cato* was carrying lumber, too, Hannah."

I nodded. He knew what was in the hold of every ship that cleared Salem Harbor. And their destinations. He talked with all the captains before they set sail.

"I know what you are thinking, Hannah," he said. "But wait, before you think it."

"I can't help it. The timing is right. Abby wrote again, a week after they arrived at Hispaniola. They sold the lumber, made a profit, and were taking on sugar and molasses. Coffee was in short supply. Nate was talking about waiting two weeks for coffee before heading back to Charleston, she wrote. That letter was written at the beginning of May."

Silence. He nodded.

"I've always known when Abby was in trouble, Parson. We've been kindred spirits. And we were so close, growing up."

"I didn't know you fancied yourself as having uncommon powers, Hannah."

Reverend Bentley never had been a Sunday pastor. He cared about his people all week. In March, right after Father had left, the master of Cabot's school died suddenly. Rather than allow the school to close, Bentley stepped in and taught the boys for the rest of the season.

"You're the one with the uncommon powers," I said. "Cabot loves school now. And I can't thank you enough for all the little expeditions you've taken him on. I didn't know what I was going to do with him after Father and Lawrence left. He felt so abandoned."

"I'm taking several of the boys out to the Neck tomorrow. We're stopping at Juniper House, where the farmer's wife will have supper. I'll have him back before dark."

The parson's nature walks were legendary. He took many a troublesome boy from Salem under his wing. But I was still worried. "Cabot wants to go to sea someday," I confided. "As much as he likes being part of your expeditions, I'm afraid he'll run off. He makes friends with so many captains who drop anchor. He's a new friend now. British. Captain Burnaby."

"All young boys want to run away to sea, Hannah. However, I shall pay special mind to it, with Cabot. But there is another matter I would discuss with you now."

I waited. I'd known something else was coming.

"You know how I feel about the slave trade. Captain Fairfield came to my house once and called me out in a duel. Because of a sermon I preached against it right before his *Felicity* set sail."

So that was it. The slave trade. It was on everyone's tongue these days. He was going to bring up Richard. And the *Prince*. Did he suspect that this was Richard's true mission? Had he found out?

"Since our legislature passed a law against it this month, anyone now caught dealing in human cargo is going against the positive law of this Commonwealth."

"You suspect Richard, don't you?"

He set his cup down. "Dear child, don't look so bestirred. I do not suspect Richard. There is terrible secrecy about his mission. But we must trust him."

I blinked. "We?"

"Yes." He smiled. "I could feel hurt that he won't speak to me of his destination. You know how interested I am in the people and governments of all the foreign lands. And how all the ships' captains bring me rare curiosities from their travels."

"Did Richard ask you to speak to me, Parson?"

"No. But I sensed he's sore afflicted that you won't trust him."

Trust. The one sentiment I prized so highly. The one I had not yet been able to give to any man.

The reverend was watching me. "He won't tell his sister or his mother his destination," I said. "He claims that its success depends on secrecy. Could that be so, Parson?"

"Mayhap. There are routes for commercial expansion that have not yet been taken by American vessels."

"Where?" I asked eagerly. "Derby's already been to Cape Town, Isle de France, and Canton."

"What comes to mind is the northwest coast of Sumatra. I've heard many a seaman speak of it."

"What's there?" I felt a thrill.

He shrugged. "Nobody knows. And if Richard Lander goes there, he'll be entering alien waters with only crude charts."

"Then Richard is taking risks. Which means he'll only have fifty percent insurance."

"Yes," the good reverend agreed, "but merchant careers are built on such risks."

I looked into my tea cup. Did Richard know something no one else knew? He'd been halfway around the world. What information had he picked up?

"Oh, Parson, if only I could be sure of what he's about!" I blurted out.

"Do I sense a tenderness of heart for him, Hannah?"

Something in the way he said it brought tears to my eyes. "I've know him all my life. I shall always have certain feelings for him."

He nodded, waiting.

"He's asked me to wait for him," I admitted. "But how can I marry anyone who is in the slave trade? Or, who won't confide in me!"

"The man does not need to be beleaguered if

he is setting out to the other side of the world, Hannah. There are dangers enough. He needs your trust. And I think you need to give it to him."

I did not reply to that. The reverend knew me better than I knew myself.

As I walked him to the door, he looked at me. "He did let one thing slip out to me. He's acting as both captain and supercargo."

A supercargo was a seagoing agent who conducted business dealings. Many were Harvard graduates.

"We were speaking of the new Customs Service likely to be brought into being, now that nine states have ratified the Constitution and it's become law. Richard said he'll have heavy Customs duties to pay when he returns. He said he would act as supercargo to cut the costs of hiring one."

I did not understand.

"So far, Hannah, such agents have sailed only on large East Indiamen. Slavers out of Salem haven't used them. After we spoke of this, he reminded me of my clergyman's duty of confidence."

"Then he would rather have people think he's running the slave route," I mused.

"Yes. To keep his real purpose secret. I think your Richard is on to a new trade route, my dear." He patted my hand. "And he needs our prayers and our trust."

There was that word again.

"Any word from your father?" he asked before leaving.

I sighed. "Only one letter and you know of that."

"Yes. The one that told of their arrival in western Pennsylvania."

"Eight weeks just to get that far. There are times, Parson, when I don't know who to worry about first."

"According to the progress of the first party that went west, they should be arriving at their destination about now. You'll be hearing soon, Hannah."

"How can you be so placid, so sure of things?" I asked. "And what's wrong with me, that I can't be? Sometimes I'm terrified, Parson."

"What makes you think I'm not?" He looked into my eyes. He was a short, rotund man, but somehow I always thought of him as tall. Perhaps because he towered with strength.

"You? Terrified?" I laughed.

He didn't. "If we have our senses about us, we all should be, Hannah," he said kindly. "But if we give in to it, we're like that crier out there, ringing our bell and walking around saying 'Lost, lost.'"

I shivered, watching him go.

"Lost, lost, lost." The crier came back down our street after the parson left. I went out to inspect my flower garden. My flowers always cheered me. The wind was picking up. I smelled the scent of rain. I went out into the street to look for Cabot.

I was in the back parlor, quilting, later that evening, and it was then that the knock came on the door. Cabot was in bed, Mattie had gone home, and Margaret was in her room, which was off the kitchen.

I was holding the blue naval officer's coat up to the light of the oil lamp. No, I had not burned it as Father had ordered. Nor did I intend to. If it was important enough for Mama to keep, it must have been dear to her for some reason. Although I did ponder on why Mama had kept it, if she had the owner arrested. Never mind, I would use it for the centerpiece of our quilt. I'd been about to take a scissor to it when the knock sounded.

I went to the front door.

It was Mr. Leonard. Wind was gusting on the street and I could tell he fancied himself a debonair figure, standing there. He bowed. "I've come to offer my condolences, Miss Hannah."

"For what?"

"Why, for the loss of the *Swamp Fox*. Word is all over town. I thought you would need comfort on such an evening."

I felt my knees buckle. "We don't know yet that it was the *Swamp Fox*."

He blinked. "You haven't heard, then?"

"Heard what?"

"My dear, I am so sorry. Several of the timbers of the ship were found, with part of the name on them. On the shore of Hispaniola."

I have always despised women who fainted. But I did exactly that. It was the only way I could remove myself from the man's terrible presence, I suppose. And from the words he flung at me like some old seaweed.

Next thing you know I was flailing my arms. When I opened my eyes, as if to swim to some safe shore, Mr. Leonard was gone. Standing over me, was Margaret.

I seemed to dip in and out of my fainting spell like a genuine spinster. Next thing I knew, Richard was there.

"Should we be sendin' for Dr. Fletcher?" Margaret asked him.

"No, no." I struggled to sit up. "I need no doctor, Margaret."

"Rum," Richard said.

Margaret fetched it and I sipped. The oil lamps cast their shadows on the walls, larger than life. Outside it was raining. A shutter banged somewhere in another part of the house. Melancholy benumbed me. Why was Cabot standing there in the shadows, staring at me like that? Why was his shirt and hair soaking wet?

"How did you get here?" I asked Richard.

"Cabot fetched me."

It was Cabot, not Margaret, who had gone for Richard, then. I held my arm out to my brother. Margaret gave him a piece of flannel cloth to dry himself with and went to put up coffee. I hugged Cabot. "You ran all the way to Mary Lander's on a night like this?" I asked.

"No. To the wharf and the *Prince*. Captain Lander's living on her now."

I looked at Richard.

He shrugged. "It's safer."

"Safer than what?"

"It doesn't matter now." He pulled up a chair. "What did he say to you? That Leonard fellow was here."

I shuddered and drew Cabot closer. "Richard, he said the *Swamp Fox* is lost. That they found timbers with her name on it. Oh, Richard, I can't bear it."

"It's all right, Hannah," Cabot was saying. "He doesn't know, for true. Nobody does."

I looked at Richard.

"Cabot is right. Nobody knows for true," Richard said. "Now, listen to me, Hannah, and listen good! Yes, there is talk around Salem, as there always is when news of a wreck reaches us. But all we have is bits and pieces of information, with nothing behind them."

My heart was racing. All I could think of was Abby and her blue eyes and freckled face. And Nate, that wonderful man with the molasses accent and the graceful ways. "What of the floating timbers?"

"I have known, many times, for ships to keep afloat with the sterns broken away," Richard said. "I've known vessels to last days in gale winds, with rudders ruined. And survivors clinging to them until another ship hoves into view."

His quiet words fell on me like warm rain. They anchored me to my senses. I gripped Cabot's hand. "Do you think such could be true, Richard?"

"I know it. I've rescued people from such circumstances. Now, will you believe me? Or do you choose to believe Leonard? The man is slime. He preys on the weaknesses of others. What other kind of man would be scouring the countryside looking for women to work in his mill?" He stood up.

I looked at him, from his sturdy boots to his white shirtfront, his hair tied back with a bit of rough rawhide. There was nothing false about Richard. A loneliness there was, but a loneliness he wanted, that he courted. It protected him from what people said, so that his own thoughts blossomed.

He was looking down at me. "Of course, that's your choice to make, Hannah, if you choose to believe me about anything." His voice was sad. And he was speaking of more than the wreck, it seemed.

"Oh, Richard, I want to believe you!"

"Set your course, then, and stick by it. As long as you hope, Hannah, they are alive. For God's sake, once in your life, trust in something!"

He was so fervent. He was begging me. And for a moment I saw the old Richard of my childhood, who had helped me through so many troublesome times. I smiled and reached for his hand. He gave it, but he did not smile.

"I will try, Richard." I looked into his eyes. I did not know what was in his mind, but in mine the years fell away like sea spray, and I was nourished by a simple belief that things could be because Richard said they were so.

He nodded. "I will get the message out that we look for word of them," he said. "It will go, ship to ship, across the waters, and we'll hear soon."

"Thank you, Richard. And thank you for coming."

He lingered a moment, looked at Cabot, then at me. "The boy should get dry and go to bed," he said.

Cabot moved to obey. Still Richard lingered, his shadow on the wall looming larger than life over us both. "Hannah," he said, "strength begets strength."

What a strange thing for a man to say. But not strange, I decided, coming from Richard. He'd been halfway around the world. He was, at once, summoning all the dark images of life at sea, and putting them to rest. I nodded.

"I have dark forebodings," I said. "Always."

"Know them for what they are," he said.

"What are they, Richard?"

"The shadowy side of your father, who never sees good in anything. The side you must learn to contain."

I stared at him in wonderment. But, yes, he was right. And only he would know. For that side of my father had touched his life, near ruined it.

He nodded, compressed his lips, watched me for a moment to see if I understood. Then so seeing, he turned. "Goodnight, Hannah, sleep well," he said. And he was gone.

In the days that followed, I did not see Richard, but I felt a strange sense of peace come over me, as if a storm inside had subsided and I had been washed clean.

I minded Richard's words about having hope. There seemed to have been something so certain about him when he said it.

I saw him only once in the following weeks. He came to call and to give me a pistol. It was an Italian pocket pistol, made heavy by a walnut stock inlaid with silver.

I now knew how to fire a gun. Cabot had taught me, as Lawrence wanted. Richard told me to keep the pistol loaded. He did not trust Mr. Leonard.

And so the days of July passed. I tended my garden, ran the house, cared for Cabot, and worked on my quilt. It was a bright, sun-washed July. Tending the garden pleasured me, but working on the quilt reminded me of my sisters. So, though I'd finished with the centerpiece, using the blue officer's jacket, I set it aside.

I visited Mary Lander's shop two afternoons a week and one day, as we were having our tea, she told me about Mrs. Dean's little girl. The child had fallen into the vault in the necessary and perished. It was the talk of Salem. Then, on top of that news came the story of Captain Allen's young son who fell from the mast of a vessel and broke his thigh.

It was not a good summer. Trouble seemed to visit Salem town, a place that could so easily make trouble welcome.

And I was worried about Cabot. I knew that when he wasn't on one of Reverend Bentley's nature walks, he was at the wharves. Was he with Richard? He spoke, often, about Richard. And he seemed to have a fondness for the British captain, Burnaby, whose ship was still at anchor because he was awaiting lumber from Maine.

One rainy day I was sitting up in Abby's empty room, being morose and watching the rain pouring down on the widow's walk.

Mattie stood in the doorway, with a tray of tea. "I've just taken bread from the oven," she said.

I sent her for another cup and bade her sit with me.

"They'll be back, Hannah," she said gently.

"I want to be brave, like your brother said I should be. But there are moments when I feel as if I'm going to perish. My life is like the pieces of my quilt, Mattie. I can't stitch it together right."

"I've always had a black hole inside me," she said.

My eyes widened. "You, Mattie?"

"Yes. All my life I've been afraid of falling into it. Richard says it's because our father shot himself when I was a child. Richard has kept me, many a time, from falling into the hole, Hannah. He knows all about it. Because he's got the black hole in him, too."

"Richard?"

"Yes. He told me of it. It's how he senses fear in others. He can, you know. I'd have died, growing up, if I didn't have Richard around."

I understood then. The fear inside me, the terror I often felt, hearkened back to losing my mother. As Richard and Mattie had lost their father. And that's how Richard had been able to name what ailed me.

I did everything I could that month of July to keep my spirits up. Reverend Bentley came to call. And he asked if I would make a record of his collection of coins that ship's masters had brought him from around the world.

I said yes, though I suspected he wanted to keep my mind and hands busy. I was so engaged, with the coins laid out on Father's desk in his library, one night at the end of July, when the knock came on the door.

It was late. After ten. Margaret and Cabot were both in bed. I had just recorded the history of a Russian coin and set it aside. I pulled open a desk drawer and lifted out the Italian pistol.

If the caller was Mr. Leonard, I would not faint this time, no matter what he came to tell me.

Chapter Eleven

The caller was not Mr. Leonard.

"Hello, Hannah. Sorry to bother you so late. I saw a light in the window."

The caller was in frontier garb. Long leggings, fringed, tied just below the knee. Deerskin boots and fringed jacket. Wide-brimmed hat with two turkey feathers decorating it. A long-handled pistol was stuck in his belt. Some wooden decoration hung from his neck. He wore a beaded pouch and a powder horn.

The caller had the look of the wild about him.

I swayed and almost did faint, seeing him. I gripped the door frame.

His hair is too wild, I found myself thinking. Too long. And it's gone reddish from the sun. His beard was even redder. His face was browned, his eyes had creases that had not been there before. Probably from squinting into the wilderness.

"Louis!" I finally got the word out.

My hand with the pistol in it dropped to my

side. My other hand passed over my eyes. Surely, when I looked again, he would not be there.

But he was.

"I'm sorry, Hannah. I should have written."

Written, yes, I thought crazily. But you did write. Asked me to marry you. I said no.

"Louis, why are you here?" I asked. "I mean, I didn't expect you. I'm sorry." I must stop babbling. Had he come home to ask me to marry him again? And go west? Dear God, what would I do now?

"Do you always answer the door with a pistol in hand?" he asked. "This isn't the frontier. What's happened? Do you expect trouble?" He stepped forward and took the pistol from me. He turned it over in his hand and looked at it.

I was about to tell him about the pistol and why I had it when I heard the noise in the dark behind him. I knew his horse was there. I could smell it.

But something else was there, too. And I could hear it.

Something was making a mewing sound. An animal? Had he brought some wild animal with him?

He stepped back into the shadows. Then he stepped forward again. "I have something to show you, Hannah."

The way he said it sent a thrill of alarm through me. He went back into the shadows and moved around there for a moment. And when he again stepped into the circle of lamplight from the house and I saw what he had, I gasped.

"Louis, what is it?"

"It's a baby, Hannah," he said gently. And then he was handing the baby to me.

I took it. It was an Indian baby, all done up in a soft doeskin wrapper. The round little face peered up at me. Curious and bright dark eyes examined my face.

Then it smiled. And I felt something in my heart give, felt some dam of resistance break inside me and some waters of feeling that I had never felt before rush through. "Oh, Louis, he's beautiful! Where did you get him?"

"She's mine," he said.

Dumbstruck, I met his eyes. And I saw the sadness in them that I had not seen a moment ago. It was a large sadness that seemed to fill his whole being. "Yours?" I asked.

"Yes, Hannah. I didn't know where else to come with her. I need someone to care for her for me. Will you do it?"

In the kitchen I lit the fire and put up some coffee. My hands had gone numb and my heart was racing. I could not think. It took all my effort to brew the coffee and go into the larder and get out some meat and bread and cheese for Louis.

I had put him in the parlor with the baby. For some reason, I wished Margaret would wake up. She would know what to do. Her room was off the kitchen. But she was a heavy sleeper.

Louis had asked me to take care of the baby for

him. What did that mean? Keep her? For a week? A month? A year? Forever?

I had not asked. I had just put one foot ahead of the other and did what came naturally, started to bring forth the makings of a repast. Food first, then talk. Life looks better on a full stomach. People become civilized when they break bread together. Margaret had taught me that.

Gingerly, I carried a tray into the parlor. Louis had set the baby down on the sofa and she was sleeping.

I put the tray down and he ate. I poured the coffee, taking some myself. I waited for him to talk.

Finally he did. "Our government has a situation on its hands with the Indians, Hannah. The Indians tell us they don't want war, just that we stay away from their side of the Ohio River. They warn of what they'll do if we don't keep our settlers south of the river."

I did not want to hear about our government or the Indians. I wanted to hear how he came to be father of an Indian baby. But I waited.

"The Northwest Ordinance more or less gave the Indians the right to penetrate white settlements, by saying we can never take Indian lands without their consent. They've been crossing the Ohio River and conducting raids. Then retreating into territory where our people are forbidden to enter and retaliate."

My hand went to my throat and I thought of

my family. "Father and Lawrence and Thankful are gone four months now," I told him. "I've had only one letter."

He smiled sheepishly. "I almost forgot, Hannah, forgive me." He reached inside his haversack, took out three letters and handed them to me. One was for Cabot, addressed in Thankful's hand. The other for me from Lawrence. And the third to Mattie from Lawrence. Nothing from Father. So he was still angry. I placed them in my lap.

"Your family is keeping well. I saw them at Campus Martius. It's a two-story, walled fort, very strong. They were on their way to Fort Harmar, which is near the new Marietta settlement. We hear Marietta is thriving. People are calling it the gateway to the richest country in the world."

"What if the Indians attack?" I asked.

"There is peace now, Hannah. Settlers are pouring in. We just hope the Indians will honor the Fort Finney treaty, which marks the Ohio River and the border between Shawnees and whites. It was never approved by the confederacy of the Northwest Indians."

I felt a sense of dread.

"And we hope," he said bitterly, "that the fool Kentuckians can be restrained from attacking the Indians." He scowled, and looked into his coffee cup. For a moment he didn't speak. When he did it was with considerable difficulty.

"It was in such an attack that this child's mother was killed. By Kentuckians. They are angry because we can't defend them. So they go on raids."

I could not believe what he was saying. "Her mother was killed by *white* people?"

"The Kentuckians attack Shawnee villages all the time. This time most of the warriors were gone. One Kentuckian sank his sword into Night Wind's skull as she fled with the baby."

"Night Wind?"

"The child's mother."

"Your wife?" I felt strange saying the word. An Indian wife! My Louis?

"Yes. She'd gone back to her village to visit with her family soon after Night Song was born." He looked across the room at the baby on the sofa.

My mind was whirling. "How terrible," I said. "To attack a mother with a babe in her arms."

"The Indians have killed plenty of our people with equal cruelty. For a while I didn't think we'd stop killing each other. But, like I said, the killing has stopped. For now."

"Louis, when was Night Song born?"

"In May."

I said nothing. In my head I was counting back the months, from May. But Louis was ahead of me.

"You turned me down, Hannah. You said no to me. I was out in the wilderness. I wanted to die, at first."

"But you met an Indian woman. And so you

didn't die," I said bitterly. "How could you, Louis?"

He met my eyes steadily. "Part of me died, Hannah," he said gravely. He said it so plain. But it was the look in his eyes that made me believe him, a look so revealing that I knew I would never forget it. Then he turned away.

For a while neither of us said anything. The tall clock in the hallway chimed the hour. He spoke again, quietly, and his words filled the room with sadness.

"I went to the Shawnee village after I heard of the attack. Somehow the baby had survived and was being cared for by an old Indian woman. I took the child with me back to camp and found a wet nurse. A white woman who'd just given birth. Her husband had been killed in an Indian attack. Ordinarily, she'd not want to nurse an Indian child but she wanted to go back to her folks in Pennsylvania. She traveled with me and nursed the child along with her own. I saw her home and came here."

I nodded.

"Will you care for the babe for me, Hannah? I'll be here a while, recruiting men. I'll be traveling through Connecticut and New Jersey. It will be at least two months."

I nodded yes. "And then what? After two months?"

"I go back with my new men."

"And the child?"

"I don't know, Hannah. I've written to my family but they've refused. I can try to visit them and talk to them in person."

"A person could learn to love a child in two months," I said.

He nodded.

"What if that happens, Louis?"

"Why don't we wait and see what happens, Hannah," he said gently. "I've learned by now not to try to outguess God."

"Well, you're gonna have to outguess that babe!"

We both turned, startled. Looming large in the doorway was Margaret, in a night wrapper, her graying hair sticking every which way out of her nightcap. Without so much as a by-your-leave, she crossed the room and picked up the sleeping babe and held it in her arms. Thank heavens! I sensed Margaret would know how to care for the child.

"Poor motherless bairn," she said. She looked at me. "And how will you be explainin' this to your father?"

"I don't know, Margaret. I haven't explained it to myself, yet. I'm still catching my breath."

She turned to Louis. "What have you been feedin' her since you parted with the wet nurse in Pennsylvania?"

So she'd heard us talking. I breathed easier. Yes, Margaret would take charge. I felt a weight lifted.

"Gruel in goat's milk. And some sugar water," he said.

"We'll have to get a wet nurse by morning. How often does she take nourishment?"

"Every few hours or so. Although once she slept through the night," Louis said. He welcomed Margaret's questions, I could see. Here was somebody who knew about babies.

"The fresh air while you traveled, most likely," Margaret said. She ran her eyes over him, up and down over his person. If she had any qualms about Louis having an Indian baby, she'd hide them, I knew. "I'd best make up some gruel for the next feedin'. I'll take her in my room this night. You'd best get some rest, young man. You look done in."

"I'll sleep in the barn," Louis said.

"You'll be doin' nothin' of the kind," Margaret scolded. "That's a perfectly good sofa. Take off your boots."

"It wouldn't be seemly," Louis protested. "Since Hannah and I were once betrothed."

"You're worried about seemly?" Margaret asked. "You, who took an Indian wife? And with what I just heard you say happened to this child's mother?"

"No, I thought you would be," Louis said.

"Son," Margaret said, "I've seen enough trouble in my lifetime to know when to worry about seemly and when not. I'll wager you've other things on your mind, besides romance, right now. And I'll wager you'll go to sleep as soon as you lay down your head."

"Thank you, ma'am, but I must bed my horse first." And Louis commenced to take off his belt and knife. Carefully, he set his pistol aside. Margaret handed me the baby and brought a pillow and a light blanket.

I gazed into the baby's face. Such long black lashes! She was beautiful! And I thought I saw some of Louis in her face, too.

Louis's baby! I still felt numb, handing her back to Margaret. Then I looked at Louis before I left the room.

He was so tall and spare, so weathered. And, as Margaret showed him through the kitchen, out the back door, and pointed to the barn, I stood and watched him take a lantern and go out into the night to bed his horse. He moves with the soft-footed sureness of an Indian, I thought. And he looks more like an Indian than a white man, too. Strange, I minded, going up the stairs. I've never *seen* an Indian. So how could he remind me of one?

The idea made me uneasy in my bones.

Before I went to bed I did two things. I crept into Cabot's room and laid the letter from Thankful next to his pillow. Then I read my letter from Lawrence.

He said that the trip west had been both uneventful and exciting at the same time, that Father was well, that Thankful was doing her chores and although she'd given him sass about doing school-work with the other children, in the end, she saw the error of her ways. He did not elaborate.

He was writing from Campus Martius. The scenery, when they'd floated down the Ohio River, had been the most beautiful he'd ever seen and he'd done some sketching.

"Several times, Hannah, we sighted whites waving from the shore, but we'd been warned of this, told not to stop, that sometimes the Indians placed white captives to wave in distress. And when the settlers stop to help, they are slaughtered."

The candlelight cast a curious light in my room as I read this. I thought of the baby downstairs, whose mother had been slaughtered by whites, and shivered.

"Father and I have little to say to each other," the letter went on, "but I don't grieve over that. My duties as second-in-command keep me too busy. And Father is busy striking deals to set up a trading post in Marietta. He hopes to lure traders from the west.

"I will write again, but if you do not hear from us, do not think the worst. The mails are undependable at best. I met with Louis and he told me of the child he is taking east, Hannah. As I give him this letter for you, I write that he has not told Father. Only me, and I shall not divulge his secret. He asked if I thought you would care for her for a while. I said yes, as you have taken care of all of us so well. I know you, Hannah. Perhaps caring for this child right now is just what you need. . . ."

I blew out my candle and fell asleep with the letter in my hand. Once, in the night, I thought I heard the baby cry from the far reaches of the house. Was it a dream?

Black holes all around me, I decided. Every time I drifted off again the sight of Louis in buckskins pulled me awake. Or I saw the Indian baby's mother being slaughtered, while running. Sometimes I saw the *Swamp Fox*, wrecked and in pieces.

My world was in pieces. Toward morning I dreamed of the settlers waving from the shores of the Ohio. Their faces were those of Nate and Abby.

In the morning I awoke to find Mattie gripping a bedpost and standing over me.

"There's a baby in the house."

"Yes, Mattie, I know."

"I go into the kitchen and Margaret is bathing it. And a man is at the table, eating breakfast. He looks like a wild man, then Margaret told me he is your Louis."

"Not mine anymore, Mattie. The baby is from an Indian wife."

She handed me my hot chocolate. I waved it aside and got out of bed. "I need strong tea. I'll get dressed and go right downstairs."

She helped me, her eyes shrewd. "It's a lovely

baby. Margaret's told me he's asked you to keep it for a while. Will you?"

I sighed. "I don't know how I can say no. He needs help. His family has refused. I should say no. He turned around and married an Indian woman."

"But you turned him aside," she reminded me gently.

Her eyes met mine fully and I minded how like Richard she was, with her maddening logic. "Did you get your letter from Lawrence? I left it on the table next to your bed last night."

Her eyes were shining. "Yes."

"And did Cabot get his from Thankful?"

"Yes, but he ran out of the house sulking. He wouldn't even eat breakfast."

I put on a morning gown and brushed back my hair and tied it with a ribbon. "Thankful must be lording it over him because she's having adventures and he isn't. I'll speak to him later. Do I look presentable?"

"More than presentable. Louis *is* handsome under all the wildness. Does this visit mean he's still sweet on you? Does my brother have competition?"

"I shall not answer that question, Mattie," I said rather sharply. "It is frivolous, in view of the problems I have this morning."

She stepped aside as I went out the door of my room. She looked properly chastened, but now her eyes had a twinkle in them.

In the kitchen Margaret was feeding the baby some gruel and cooing to her. As I came into the room, she stopped cooing. "Is he going to let us baptize her or does he want her raised a heathen?" she asked.

I sighed and reached for a cup of tea. More questions. Why did everyone think I had all the answers? "I don't know," I said wearily.

"Well, ye'd best be askin'. He's out there, readyin' to leave. Get that clear, Miss Hannah, before he goes. And ask when he'll be fixin' to return, so's we're not burdened with the bairn forever."

I took my tea outside, walked through my garden. As soon as the door closed, I heard Margaret cooing to the child again. Burdened with the child? Margaret didn't fool me for an instant.

It was a fine day, blue sky, warm sun dappling shadows through the trees. My flowers were all in bloom. They nodded to me in the faint breeze, like friends.

Our barn was on the far side of the garden gate. There stood Louis, talking with John Gardener, son of our widowed neighbor. John cared for the carriage horses and grounds, ofttimes drove our carriage, and was a general all-around man. He nodded politely to me.

"The man knows of a woman who may act as wet nurse," Louis said. "His sister just had a baby."

"That's right, I'd forgotten, John," I said. "But would your sister do it? Not everyone would."

"I'll ask, Miss Hannah."

I was left alone with Louis. His horse was saddled, his supplies all packed on. "You're leaving." I said it like an accusation.

"I must be on my way, Hannah." He smiled at me. It was the same smile I'd learned to hang my heart on before he'd gone west. And for a moment I hung my heart on it again.

"You'll take care of the child for me, then?"

"I suppose I will," I said. "Don't I do for everyone?"

"Don't be angry with me, Hannah. I couldn't abide it."

"What about me, Louis? How can I abide taking care of another woman's child every day? Have you thought of that?"

"Yes," he said softly.

"And?"

"I've thought that you'd do it because you once loved me. And because, if you hadn't said no to me, it would be our child. Only because you said no is she someone else's, Hannah."

"I accept that, Louis, because I have to."

He nodded. "You set the course for us, Hannah, not I. I didn't turn you aside for another."

"I don't blame you for that."

"What do you blame me for then?"

I looked into his face, once so dear to me. "For being a man, Louis, I suppose."

"I accept that, Hannah," he said humbly.

I nodded. There was no more to say. Words rose

in my throat and died. To what end, my anger? He was going away. I might never see him again. What of *that*? What if he never came back? But I could not give voice to the matter.

He, too, was struggling to give voice to some matter. Finally he did. "You may have trouble here in Salem. You should be ready for it. People most places don't accept a half-Indian child. In Salem they can be downright small-minded. A lot of people here have sent kin out west."

"What are you saying, Louis?"

"That if anything happens to any of our people out there, the town may turn against the child. And you, for harboring her."

"Blame a baby? How dare they? Especially when she's the child of a man who's on the frontier protecting our settlers," I demanded. "Shouldn't that count for something?"

A slow smile spread across his face. "So you'd fight for her, then?"

"You know I would!" It came to me then what he was doing, forging a bond between me and the child. Or assuring himself that one could be forged, if need be.

"You needn't play on my feelings, Louis," I said. "Or worry. I'll care for the child as if she were mine."

"It's what I wanted to hear, Hannah. Thank you."

We said our goodbyes. He did not go back into

the house. He gave me permission to christen the child and left the choice of name to me.

Before he mounted his horse he looked over my shoulder with that far-reaching gaze of his that had so often scanned mountains. "Your brother has some trouble on his mind this day," he cautioned. "He barely said hello. I know he remembers me from Philadelphia."

I followed his gaze. And there, far across the garden I saw Cabot behind some trees.

"Cabot!" I waved. But he dashed away.

"I'll take my leave now Hannah. I'll be back soon."

I watched him ride away, then went back into the house. Margaret had sent Mattie up to the garret for the old cradle. Margaret thrust the child into my arms and asked me to hold her. She was going out with John Gardener, to speak to his sister and ask her to be a wet nurse. "I dinna know what's possessed Cabot," she said. "But he's run off."

I was left alone in the kitchen, the baby in my arms. I didn't even have breakfast yet, I sulked, and nobody cared. Cabot was out running around somewhere, with some trouble on his mind, and I must attend to it.

With the child in my arms I reached for a slice of freshly baked bread, poured myself another cup of tea. Mattie called down from upstairs, asking what linen to use in the cradle and I yelled an answer back up.

Confusion reigned. There was a baby in the house. I looked down at her in my arms. Her little fists curled into balls as if to fight off the world. Why, I thought, she has Louis's eyes! Was that possible?

I thought of what Louis had said about the possibility of the townfolk turning against her. I felt her warmth against me, her softness, and hugged her, feeling a fierce protectiveness. "I won't let any harm come to you," I said.

She looked up at me, directly into my eyes, listening. And it was as if she understood.

And then she smiled at me. And in that moment, before her father had even reached the outskirts of Salem town, my fate was sealed with hers, forever.

Chapter Twelve

To put it in Margaret's words, I dinna know what possessed Cabot either. But I was too busy all morning to think of him. Mattie brought old baby clothing down from the attic. I sorted them out and she washed them. Then, around noon, Margaret came back with the wet nurse. Yes, she would nurse the child, she said. We insisted upon paying her. It would not be easy, in Salem, to get another to do so. Not with a half-Indian baby.

It wasn't until I was alone in the dining room, taking lunch, that I thought to ask Mattie about Cabot. Her only answer was to lay a note on the table beside my plate.

It was the letter that had come to Cabot from Thankful. Quickly, I read it.

Dear Cabot: Since Lawrence said I had to write to you, I am determined it not be a waste of time. I have had many adventures so far. And it is so good to be away from school and horrible Hannah. Does she still make you go to bed at eight every night? Many nights I have sat up late around the campfire, hearing stories about Indians from the scouts who have made this trip before.

Father purchased one of the best horses for me in Pennsylvania, so it has been my privilege to ride at Father's side. We have many agreeable talks and he confides in me.

And that is why I am writing. It is my sad duty to report to you something Father told me one night, late, around the campfire. He said you are not his son.

He'd had some rum. And you know he can't hold his liquor, any more than Lawrence can. He talked, first, about how Abby disappointed him. And how Hannah betrayed him by helping her elope. And how Lawrence failed him by not wanting to become a merchant.

Then he told me how that awful British officer was welcomed into our house by Mama when the war was on and he was away. Oh, Cabot, he was crying! Mama betrayed him, he said with the man who once owned that blue officer's coat I gave Hannah. How terrible! I thought the owner of that coat caused trouble only because Mama fed him. Oh, I hope Hannah throws the coat out, I do. And Father also told me that Abby is just like Mama and that's why she ran off with the first man in trousers who asked her. He said I was his comfort, the only child after his heart.

Well, Cabot, you always knew he didn't like you, but you never knew why. I think it's better you be advised. God help me, he said, but I can't abide the boy most of the time.

He said your real father is a seaman and that's why you're so daft about the sea. I know you'll thank me someday for telling you this, Cabot. I have never been fond of you myself, but I know you have sufficient spirit not to want to sit around looking to a father who isn't about to be one to you. At least now you know it isn't your real father who doesn't love you.

I must get to bed now. I am dispatching this with Louis, Hannah's old beau who is making a trip back east. I must say he is dashing and Hannah was a fool to have turned him down. But she never had the sense God gave a goose, anyway. Good luck to you Cabot, whatever you decide to do. Your sister, Thankful.

My hands were trembling. I looked up at Mattie. "You read this?"

"Yes," she whispered, "but I was hoping . . ."

I was out of my chair like a shot. "Get my shawl, quickly."

"Where are you going, Hannah?"

"Going?" I grabbed my reticule, stuffed the note in it, took the light summer shawl and draped it around me, more to girth myself in strength than for warmth. "Going? I don't know. To find Cabot."

"I'll come with you."

"No."

"Yes. Margaret can stay with the baby. I feel responsible. I should have given you the note sooner."

We went out the side door of the house. "Where?" I asked her as we cut through the front yard and across Derby Street. But I knew, and so did she. To the wharves.

I followed Mattie instinctively, allowing her to lead. My head was reeling with the memory of Thankful's spidery scrawl on that paper.

One night, late, around the campfire he said you are not his son.

My mind stopped at those words as if I'd run aground, dashed myself on some rockbound coast. *And then, he told me how that awful British officer was welcomed into our house by Mama when the war was on.*

I thought of Mama. No, no. My mind threw off any such betrayal by her. She would not do such. Doxie, my father had called her. But, rushing through the summer dusk behind Mattie, I knew, as sure as I knew there was a God, that if indeed the British officer was Cabot's father, Mama was not at fault. My father had been through the war. Hadn't he heard the whispered tales of the British forcing themselves on American women? Even I'd heard such stories.

But then why did she save his coat? The question haunted me, and I felt my faith in Mama caving in. Could she have done such a thing? I minded the night of the storm when I was a little girl, when the British officer came back, how I'd peeked downstairs and seen him in the front hallway, heard his voice in spite of the storm, how, the next morning when I asked Mama why he had left, she said he'd never come back and I must have been dreaming.

She had lied to me. He *had* come back. Was Father right about her then? I had no time to think on it now. I had to find Cabot.

Where was Mattie taking me? We were walking down Derby, along the wharves. We'd passed Captain Ingersoll's house and wharf, White's Wharf, and were heading to Orne's Wharf. I was breathless. The tide was going out. I could smell the docks and water in the summer afternoon. We passed Orne's and were coming to Becket's shipyard.

And the *Prince*. I might have known. Mattie was taking me to her brother. I stopped and grabbed her hand. "Why here? I don't need Richard now. Why does everybody think he can remedy all my ills?"

She spoke to me as to a child. "Because he'll know where Cabot is, Miss Hannah. Come now."

Dumbly, I followed her. The *Prince* was resting in the water of Salem's harbor, the tide was fast going out. On the wharf were men bearing arms and standing guard. I stopped to stare at them. "Mattie, what's going on?"

"Richard has to post guards. Most of them are

his crew. People have been threatening him because of the rumor of the slave trade."

"Oh, Mattie, I didn't know."

"One night a crowd came here and pelted the *Prince* with eggs and dung and rocks. That's why he's been living on her. It's all right, come on, these men know me. They'll let us aboard."

Sometimes I think that all of us in our family had been moving toward some terrible moment for years. Probably since 1775 when those British warships weighed anchor off Salem's coastline and those British officers came into our house.

As I stood with Mattie, looking at the *Prince*, it came to me that things had been going on all around me for a while of which I was not sensible. Things from which Richard and perhaps even Mattie and others had been protecting me.

It also came to me that I was about to find out, this day, what those things were.

We went up the gangway to board the ship. It was fully restored. Richard had done a wonderful job. The *Prince* was a three-masted square-rigger now, built for speed, polished, and reinforced and heavily armed to protect herself. I could see by the way she'd been rebuilt that she had lots of precious cargo space. I knew, from being my father's daughter, that profits were made by packed holds.

And I could see from the faces of the men guarding her that Richard had selected a crew that seemed most resolute and capable.

One of his men fetched him. He came forward, saw us, and frowned. "Hannah?" He looked from Mattie to me. "What's wrong?" he asked.

"We can't find Cabot. Oh, Richard, you've got to help!" Mattie started pouring out the story. I took Thankful's letter from my reticule and gave it to him. He held up a hand to silence his sister and read it. I waited, catching my breath and taking comfort from his strong presence.

"This is terrible." He looked at me.

I nodded.

"To think that this child would write such to her own brother." He shook his head and handed the note back to me.

"I must find him, Richard. Have you seen him? Early this morning Margaret told me he ran out of the house sulking."

"Why didn't you go after him then?" He looked at me sternly. I shook my head. "There's too much to tell now, Richard. Have you *seen* him?"

"Yes. He was here earlier. I thought he was acting strange. I invited him to eat a noon meal with me. He never turns down food. But he refused. Said he had business with the captain of the *Neptune*. I thought naught of it."

"The *Neptune?*"

"Yes. It's a British East Indiaman. Captained by Burnaby. Cabot made friends with him last time he was in port."

We stood there, the three of us, ruminating. From the distance I heard the town watch crying the hour in Salem. A bell chimed from somewhere on the ship. Two times. And I heard the lapping of the outgoing tide against her sides. I felt strangely removed from everything, yet at the same time tied to Mattie and Richard by the same confusion.

Richard stared at me. "Dear God," he said. "Burnaby."

"What?" I asked.

He shook his head as if to dismiss the thought. "Never mind. The *Neptune* sailed out to the channel half an hour ago. But she's 330 tons and 99 feet long. Sluggish, like all East Indiamen. She can't make nine knots off-the-wind. But she's got the outgoing tide."

Then, to himself, he muttered, "And so do we." He drew himself up. "Hannah, I promised you a trip on the *Prince*'s maiden voyage. Are you ready?"

Mattie was shaking her head vigorously, smiling. I stared at Richard, not taking his meaning. "You mean now?"

"Yes. There's a fair breeze. We can catch the *Neptune* within the hour."

"But how can you be sure Cabot is on her?"

He'd already shouted to summon his men aboard. They came, crowded around him. "All hands to make sail," he ordered. "And look alive."

They scattered to their stations. From the corner

of my eye I saw them all over the place, moving to Richard's orders while he yelled, "Topmen aloft," and "To the jib," and "We need the wind at our nose," and "Release the gaff tackle."

He stood on deck, barking orders, one minute staring up into the bright blue sky as his men climbed up the shrouds to get to the masts. They stumbled and swore. I heard the squeaking of winches, felt the southeasterly wind begin to fill the sails.

Then the *Prince* moved. For the first time since the end of the war. Tears came to my eyes. Overhead her sails filled with wind, like angels' wings.

"Up anchors!" Richard shouted. A man ran to cut the bowline, and Richard sliced the aft-anchor line with his sword. He was using not only the wind but the currents and outgoing tide. As he strode past me to grasp the tiller, I grasped his sleeve. "Richard, how do you know Cabot is on the *Neptune*?"

"Because Burnaby told me he'd come ashore in Salem when he captained a British ship during the war. And was arrested."

He did not look at me as he said this. It was then that I realized he'd known about Mother and the Britisher all along.

"Mattie? Take her below deck and find her some rum. She looks as if she needs it. And secure my things," he said.

In the captain's cabin, Mattie found the rum and poured a glass for me. I was shaking. Mattie then started doing Richard's bidding. She took everything off his desk, stored his books, maps, sextant, and other belongings in sturdy cabinets. She made everything secure.

I watched her. She was so sure of herself, like Richard. Why wasn't I like that?

"What's happened to my life, Mattie?" I asked her. "I feel as if it's blown apart in my face. I don't know if Nate and Abby are alive. There's a half-Indian baby in my house I'm looking after for a man I was once betrothed to. My sister Thankful has unearthed an awful family story, and I'm on my father's old privateer, about to race through the water to bring Cabot back from a man he's run off with who may be his real father."

Mattie locked a cabinet and turned to give me a sad smile.

"Did you and Richard know, all along, that Cabot had a different father?" I asked.

"I didn't. But I think Richard and my mother knew."

Mary. Of course. And she'd never told me. Richard and Mary had kept it from me. I felt conspired against.

"I'm sure Richard wanted to spare you the pain," she said in answer to my unasked question.

"But Burnaby was in port. And Cabot made friends with him. Why didn't Richard do something?"

She shook her head. "I don't think Richard knew it was Burnaby. He's just become sensible of it. My mother, most likely never told him who Cabot's father is."

I looked out the small windows in the cabin. The wharves of Salem were receding, the shoreline and houses fast disappearing. We were at sea. I could feel the *Prince* cutting through the waters. The rum warmed my bones and soon I stopped shaking. Mattie came to sit beside me.

"Suppose we don't catch up with the *Neptune?*" I asked. "I can't lose Cabot."

"This ship is built for speed," she said.

Just as she said that we heard footsteps coming down the companionway, then outside the door. Richard came in. "We've got a good wind. Ought to be alongside the *Neptune* soon." He was wearing oilskins.

"Will Burnaby let us aboard?" I asked.

"Let me worry the matter."

"He's Cabot's father, isn't he?"

"So it would seem."

"Did you know this?"

"No, Hannah. I've only spoken with the man once or twice. Not until you showed me the letter did I connect it with what he once told me."

"Your mother and my father hate each other, Richard," I said, "with good reason, I suppose. But they're alike, keeping secrets from their children."

He nodded. "That generation that came through the war has a lot of secrets to keep," he said.

"Do you think Burnaby knows he's Cabot's father?"

Richard shook his head. "He might be mindful of it, if Cabot's given his right name."

"Then he's taken Cabot."

"Abducted?" Richard shook his head no. "I hope not. It's a serious offense. I curse myself for not paying mind to the boy earlier today, but I had another visit from a group of indignant Salem citizens, intent on harming the *Prince*. We'll bring Cabot back, Hannah. Calm yourself."

I nodded.

"Mattie, you'll find oilskins in the port closet, just aft of the galley," he directed.

She went out to get them.

"Hannah, you can come with me in the skiff and board the *Neptune* if you wish. I'm going to try to keep this as amicable as possible, unless the man gives us trouble. I don't think he will."

"Thank you, yes, I'll come along."

"You have to decide if you want Cabot to know who Burnaby is," he said.

My eyes went wide. "What makes you think he hasn't already told Cabot?"

He shook his head. "Cabot's known him a while. He doesn't seem to me to be the sort who wants the responsibility of a son. I think he's playing with the boy, enjoying him from a distance. Do you want some advice?"

"Yes, of course."

"Don't tell Cabot, if Burnaby hasn't. Not today. You'll never get your brother home if you do."

I nodded and thanked him. Mattie came back with the oilskins and we put them on and went above deck. The air was full of salt spray. The *Prince* was cutting smoothly through the water, foaming spume splashing up at the sides. Richard took his place at the tiller. And, as he had promised, within the half hour, we were on a parallel course with the majestic, but laboring *Neptune*.

I shall remember that day as long as I live. There was something at once dreadful and magical about it. As I sat in the skiff with Richard and the two rowers, the hulking sides of the *Neptune* coming closer, I drew my oilskins about me and minded that I was about to meet the man with whom my mother had had a child.

The man who had come into my mother's life and ruined it. I looked up at the vast sky as our skiff cut through the water between the two ships. Until now, I hadn't known this man existed, except as some phantom object of my father's hatred. And as the owner of the blue British naval officer's coat that now served as the centerpiece of my quilt.

This was the person who was responsible for my family being torn into pieces. I felt a strange sense of destiny, sitting in that skiff. As if I were stitched to both the past and the future now, going to meet this man, as firmly bound to both as that piece of blue fabric was to my quilt.

I felt close to my mother. I looked across the small boat at Richard. Bound I was to him, too, now. For he was the person taking me on this strange mission.

Richard's face was solemn. He'd removed his oilskins before leaving the *Prince* and put on a fresh white shirt, ruffle and stock at the throat. He was wearing a good coat and tricorn hat and he'd buckled on his sword. Under the coat, I saw a pistol stuck in his belt. Dear God, did he expect trouble?

"Launch alongside!" The voice came from overhead. Then, "Stand off there. And identify yourselves!"

A young man was standing at the starboard rail of the *Neptune*, looking down at us.

"Captain Richard Lander of the *Black Prince*, out of Salem," Richard said, standing up. "We've business with Captain William Burnaby."

"State your business."

"Respectfully, I refuse to state it to anyone but your captain," Richard shouted up.

In a moment another man came to the rail. He stood a little behind the first officer, and I could not see his face. But his voice cut through the salt-sprayed air, clipped and British and authoritative.

"Captain Lander! Good day. I wasn't expecting company."

"Permission to come aboard with Miss Hannah

Chelmsford," Richard called up. "Do you have Cabot Chelmsford aboard? We've reason to believe he's run off. He's her brother."

"Permission to come aboard, Captain Lander," Burnaby said.

William, I thought. His name is William: It's Cabot's middle name. Who had done *that*! Certainly not Father.

"Do you know who the boy is?" Richard's face was masked with severity, his eyes hard as he leaned across the wide walnut table to look at Burnaby.

The captain had ordered tea and cakes for us. He had been most pleasant, bowed when introduced to me, but never looked me in the eyes as he ushered us into his cabin.

"Do I know who he is?" He stirred his tea with a silver spoon, set the spoon down, and sipped. "That depends on who is doing the asking. If the boy asks, I tell him he is the son of Nathaniel Chelmsford, well-known Salem merchant. If you ask, well, my answer could be different. And if the young lady here asks . . . " He smiled at me. But the smile had nothing to do with the look in his eyes, which still did not meet mine. "Well, if the young lady here asks, I don't know yet what my answer should be."

"She knows," Richard said.

"Ah." Burnaby sighed. "Which accounts for the way she is looking at me."

"If she is looking at you in any particular way," Richard enunciated carefully, "it is because she is worried sore about her brother."

"No need to worry," Burnaby said.

"No need? Captain, you are forcibly detaining aboard a foreign merchant vessel a young man who is a minor and the son of one of Salem's foremost citizens. I'd say you had every reason to worry."

But Burnaby was not concerned. "Come now, Lander, I'm not forcibly detaining anybody. The lad's been poking around my ship since I first dropped anchor in Salem. We became quite fast friends. As he's made friends with many other ships' captains who frequent your port."

"The difference being," Richard said evenly, "that other ships' captains don't abduct him."

"I've abducted nobody." Burnaby stood up to open a cabinet. He took out a crystal decanter, poured some dark liquid into his tea, and offered some to Richard, who waved it aside.

He was a tall man with a good breadth to his shoulders. Not young, no. There was gray hair at his temples, but the hair was still full. And though he was no youth anymore, there was a leanness about him, an agility that bespoke youth. He wore a black coat of good cut, his linen was spotless, his manner cultured.

He sat down again and smiled across the table at me. My heart thudded. It was an *endearing* smile. Something boyish in it. He was a handsome man. Had he then, indeed, captured my mother's fancy?

"I have not abducted your brother, Miss Hannah," he said gently. "He was running away and asked me to take him aboard. He'd have found someone else to run off with, if I didn't take him under wing. I intended, full well, to return him in the morning."

"In the morning?" My voice croaked.

"Yes. I was taking him up the coast this evening. We were to sup together. He told me how he wants to go to sea. How his father went west and did not take him."

"Did he tell you anything else?" I asked.

"Yes." He smiled wryly. "He told me about the letter he received from his sister, informing him that Nathaniel Chelmsford is not his father. And how the man feels about him. Poor little beggar."

"And what did you say to that, Captain Burnaby?" I demanded.

"I told him I didn't know who my father was, either."

My eyes narrowed. "A British naval officer needs to be commissioned by his monarch," I said. "One doesn't get such a commission with such a background."

"You are correct, Miss Hannah. I had a patron. My stepfather. A most wonderful man who knew the right people. I apologize for causing you worry. I shouldn't have taken the boy. I knew I could get into trouble. But then, there are many things I should not have done in my life. I admit that to you eagerly. I'll have him sent for in a few moments, and you, sir," he said to Richard, "can ask him if we haven't agreed, he and I, that he's to go back in the morning."

"We'll be taking him back this day," Richard nodded. "Save you the time."

"As you wish. But also, please let me say that this little jaunt this afternoon gave me a chance to get to know the boy. He's bright as a newly minted shilling. Knows enough to be a midshipman already. Given the way your father feels about him, Miss Hannah, can you expect the man to educate the boy? Even in his own counting house?"

"My father will educate him," I said. "I'll see to it."

"He told me he refuses to take anything from his father!"

"I'll educate him," Richard said. "I'll take him to sea."

"He'll run away to sea himself, first," Burnaby said.

"Wait a minute, both of you!" I said. "Must this be decided right now?"

"No, but since we're not likely to meet again, Miss Hannah, I'd like to make an arrangement to pay for the boy's education."

My head was spinning. I was benumbed with weariness. I could not reply.

"With what conditions?" Richard asked.

"You decide. He needn't know who I am unless

you choose to let him know. The money can be sent to Miss Hannah. But she should tell him there will be money for his schooling that isn't his father's."

Richard nodded at me.

"Thank you, Captain," I said. "But there is one thing I must know first, before I have anything more to do with you."

He smiled. "You American girls are so forthright."

"Yes, we are. And I shall expect forthrightness from you now in return. I would ask you something."

The blueness of his eyes deepened. From somewhere in the bowels of the ship I heard four bells chime. "Did my mother have you and your men arrested that night so long ago?"

"She did." His smile was downward curved, wry.

"But you came back later."

"I did."

"Why?"

"I talked myself out of the arrest. I can be very persuasive, Miss Chelmsford." His eyes were saying things to me. They were warm and smiling. *What were they saying?*

"Was my mother expecting you?"

"She was not."

"Did she receive you, then? Welcome you?"

His eyes got a faraway look in them. And there was no one else in that cabin with us then. It was as if Richard were not there. Only Captain William Burnaby and myself. And the ghost of my mother.

"She did not welcome me, Miss Hannah. At first."

I felt my mouth go dry. "At first?"

"Dear child," and he reached across the table as if to take my hand.

I drew it back. "Tell me," I said.

He gave a heavy sigh. "She did not welcome me at first. But I was quite taken with her. I could not get her out of my mind, though she had had me arrested. Such spirit! Your mother was a lovely woman, in many ways. She ordered me out, as a matter of fact. But I was quite charming in those days."

"Did you force yourself on her?"

He looked at me as if I'd lost my senses for a moment. Then he answered. "Dear girl, I did not! I would not commit such an abomination!"

"Then what happened?"

He smiled. "We talked. She had quite a tongue and wit. We talked for hours, after she let me stay. And I found out the marriage had been an unhappy one for the last few years."

"Then you are saying that my mother gave herself to you? Willingly?"

"My dear, she was lonely and sore afflicted and fair starved for kindness. Your father was a precious bad husband."

"And you were precious good to her."

"I tried to be, yes."

"And then you left."

"We managed, oh, one or two more meetings. Then I left, yes. I was summoned to duty. I made her no promises. She made none to me."

"Did you know you had a son with my mother?"

"No, I never suspected until I came back to Salem. And he told me who he was and how old he was. And then I knew when he told me of the letter."

I felt a ringing in my ears, like the roaring of water. *My mother had willingly given herself to this man.* I could not fathom the thought. Was my father right then in what he said of her? Was she like a doxie?

I bent my head over the table. My breath came with difficulty.

"Hannah," I heard Richard say. I felt his hand on my arm, shook him off.

"Miss Hannah," came the voice of Burnaby, "look at me."

I looked.

"Your mother was a lady. I held her in highest esteem. I am eternally in debt for the short time I was privileged to know her. It was no mere dalliance. She haunted me for years afterward. I came back to Salem five years ago to seek her out. Only then did I learn that she'd died."

I just stared at him.

"She loved your father true, she told me. She took that love as far as it could go, 'til she could take it no further. 'Twas he who killed it, not she. And not I."

Still I said nothing.

"Do you know why she locked us in the root cellar and had us arrested?"

"Because she was a Patriot," I said.

"Because she felt her heart quicken toward me when she fed us supper. She wanted me out of the way."

Richard smiled. "That's why every good American household has a root cellar," he said.

"Don't, Richard," I said.

"Come, Hannah, the man is being truthful with you. He is baring his soul. Have mercy on him," Richard murmured.

"You asked me to be forthright, Miss Hannah," Burnaby said. "I thought you could abide it. Perhaps I should tell you one more thing, however, to keep you from thinking harshly of your mother."

Tears crowded my eyes. What would he tell me next?

"Your father beat her on occasion," he said. "She was glad the war took him away. He had demons in him, she told me. She endured it. But prayed he would not come back from the war."

I felt slapped. For a moment I could not breathe. I felt Richard's arm around my shoulder and I leaned into it. Dear God, I prayed, be good to my mother.

He stood and we eyed each other across the table. I took his full measure for an instant. He smiled at me. It was more like a blessing. His blue eyes were pools of kindness. I wished I could jump into them and lose myself. Is this what Mama had seen?

"Thank you, Captain," I said. "I accept your offer to educate my brother. Richard will make arrangements with you. Now tell me where Cabot is so I may see him."

He bowed, took my hand and kissed it. The man had charm. I was not immune to it. But I wanted to leave the room as quickly as I could.

I found Cabot reading in a hammock below deck, where twenty or so hammocks were gently swinging. He was not surprised to see me, he'd seen us hove into view. He came amiably. I did not scold, but told him that I loved him, no matter what Thankful had said, and that Richard and I would always hold him dear to us.

"I used the sextant, Hannah," he said. "Captain Burnaby was surprised that I knew how. He was going to let me stand watch later. He said I'm ahead of most boys my age, knowing about the sea."

"That is a compliment," I said.

"I want to go to sea, Hannah. Before Father comes home." He stood looking up at me, straight-backed and slender, a child no longer, the day's events having turned him into a man. "I don't want to be underfoot when he comes home. You must let me go, please."

We went above deck. I put my arm around him. "You must finish school and go to college. Then you can become a supercargo."

"That takes money and I want none from Father."

"Don't worry, the money will come from somewhere."

He stopped and looked up at me. "Perhaps I can work for Richard someday?"

"Yes, perhaps."

"Have you told him about the baby, Hannah? I saw her this morning."

I stopped. I'd forgotten about the baby. Yes, I must tell Richard.

"If you want to keep her, I'll help mind her," Cabot said.

In the launch on the way back to the *Prince*, I held Cabot, fused by a new, fierce, and protective love for him. It was then that I determined that Cabot would have the best education. And if Father or Thankful dared disparage him when they came home, they would answer to me.

Richard and I did not speak in the launch. There was no need to. Aboard the *Prince* again, he bade me and Cabot and Mattie to go below deck and rest. But we were not tired.

"We'll stay out of the way while you bring her about," Cabot begged.

Richard agreed. So the three of us sat on the quarterdeck, wrapped in blankets, and watched.

And Cabot explained how Richard was turning the *Prince*.

"Much precision and work is necessary to turn her," he said. "First they're trimming the yards close to the axis of the hull. See? They're also hauling in the sheet of the fore and aft driver, so it's taut on the mizzenmast so as to kick her stern around."

"Ready and about!" someone shouted.

"That's Richard's first mate," Cabot explained. "His name is Corbett."

Richard was at the wheel.

"He's turning hard," Cabot said, "all the way to starboard, to put the helm, which connects to the rudderhead, to leeward."

"Helm's hard a-lee," Richard shouted.

"Now the men are letting go the jib and staysail sheets to trim the headsails," Cabot told us. "The rudder will bring the ship into the southeasterly wind. See? The yards are pointed into it."

We saw. The sails shivered and the lines danced, free in the wind.

"Now," Cabot shouted, "the *Prince*'s head is passing through the eye of the wind. She's heading southeast by south."

"What order did Richard just give?" Mattie asked.

"To haul taut the port jib and staysail sheets. Now, with the other foresails, they'll be back-winded, blown against the mast, and act as levers to throw her bow away from the wind and on a new course."

Mattie and I stood. I stared in amazement at Cabot, surprised at what he knew. So, all those days spent on the wharves hadn't been for naught. He seemed born to the sea.

I could feel the wind catching the starboard edge of the square mainsail, could see the sails catch the wind from the port side. Cabot was explaining it to Mattie.

"If everything isn't done at the right moment, the *Prince*'s headway could have been lost. But everything was done right."

He plopped down on the deck beside us. "That's what I want to do. Be a ship's master," he said.

The *Prince* was taking us home. We arrived back in port near dusk. Richard spoke softly to Mattie and she and Cabot proceeded to walk home. We lingered on the quarterdeck, savoring the completeness of the moment.

"How will you keep after what Burnaby told you?" he asked.

"I'll keep," I said. "Though I've much to ponder. You know, Richard, when he mentioned that my father beat my mother, it came to me. There were nights, as a child, that I recollect her crying. Once, I recollect, she had a bruise on her face."

"Damn his soul," Richard said.

We looked at each other, content in each other's company, sensible of the fact that we'd come a long way together today and it had brought us closer.

"I told you that I'd take you on the *Prince*'s maiden voyage, didn't I? She's sharp and smart. If I had any doubts about her they've been assuaged this day," he said.

If I'd had any doubts about Richard they'd been assuaged this day, too. I felt a new warmth toward him. He had placed himself, his ship, and his crew at my service without question. And seen me through my ordeal with Burnaby with determination and dash and gentle guidance.

"A ship's only as good as her master," I said.

His eyes widened. And I felt something sweet in the moment working favorably for us. "Does this mean you've had a change of heart about me?"

"I don't know what it means, Richard."

"Oh, Hannah, don't tell me you aren't mindful of the ebb and flow between us."

"I thought it was just that I was beholden to you for fetching Cabot," I teased.

"It's more. You know full well. If you'll not shut your eyes to it."

"Richard," I blurted out, "I know your ship is no slaver. I was wrong ever to think such. And my eyes are not shut. I am much taken with you this day. The *Prince* is beautiful and fast and you are as fine a master as a ship ever had."

His eyes went tender. "Are you saying you'll wait for me, Hannah?"

"I don't know your destination, Richard. And I won't ask you to tell me, again. But I do know it must be unchartered waters, that there will be risks. But I'll wait."

"Oh, Hannah." He took my hands in his own. We drew closer. I knew he was going to kiss me, but I held him off.

"There's just one thing you should know, Richard. It may get in the way of things."

"Nothing you tell me can do that."

"Listen, please. Louis came home yesterday. On a visit. He brought a baby with him. It's his, but it's half-Indian. He's here for a while, recruiting men. He's asked me to care for the baby for him. I said yes."

He stood back a bit and peered down at me. "Half-Indian! Dear God! What are you telling me then? Surely not that you still care for Louis?"

"I shall always care a bit for Louis. But I love you. However, I want to take care of the baby. I couldn't tell you before this, there wasn't time."

He nodded. "He's going back out west?"

"Yes."

"Are you saying you want to raise the child?"

"He hasn't asked me, but I don't think it will come to that. A few months, a year, at the most."

For one terrible moment I thought he was going to object. Then he smiled, wryly. "If you want this, yes, Hannah. I'll be gone a year. Perhaps this child is a godsend, to keep you from worrying."

Then he scowled. "I'd marry you before I leave, Hannah, but I haven't anything to offer you. I want to sail back into Salem Harbor with my fortune in my hold. You must let me do that, and wait."

"Yes," I said. For I knew he'd be no husband without that chance.

And so then he kissed me. A proper kiss, such as I'd never had before, not even from Louis. Right there on the *Prince*. For a moment the world was mine. I clung to him, wanting to laugh and cry all at the same time. For, in the same moment as I found my place in the world, I knew I stood a chance of losing it.

Is this what love is then? I asked myself. Knowing that once you gave in to it, the terrible knowledge that you could lose it, was always with you? Is this why Abby went to sea with Nate? Is this what my mother lost? And found, so briefly, with Burnaby?

I was interrupted in my musings by a man who came running up the gangway, waving a paper in his hand. "Captain Lander!" The man was breathless from his exertions. He saluted as he approached Richard.

"Captain Lander, sir. Compliments from Captain Benjamin Wilkes of the *Henrietta*. We're just in from Haiti."

Richard returned the salute, took a folded note and a sealed letter from him. For a moment his face froze in disbelief, as he read the note. "When?" he asked sharply.

"We met with the *Suffolk* two weeks ago, sir, in the South Atlantic. She was homeward bound, to Richmond, from the Canaries. We were a bit off course. Bad weather, sir. My captain hailed her because we heard you were looking for survivors of the *Swamp Fox*."

"Yes," Richard snapped.

The man paused to catch his breath, glanced at me, removed his hat, and nodded. I was so anxious that I wanted to leap on him to make him continue. "End of May, sir, after the storm, *Suffolk* met the *Swamp Fox*, crawling along the coast in the Caribbean. The storm had wrapped itself around the *Fox* for a week. Several of her timbers were torn off. The *Suffolk* stood by all night and through the next morning to rescue those on board. Took them aboard. Salvaged what they could, but the *Fox* went under, sir."

I let out a small cry, then covered my mouth.

"The *Suffolk* went on with her voyage to the Canaries. Got there the second week in June. Left the survivors there to recuperate, sir."

My heart was racing. Richard smiled at me and handed me the battered and sealed letter, smudged with fingerprints. And there was Abby's delicate scrawl. My name on it. In ink. My heart slammed in my breastbone. "Miss Hannah Chelmsford," it said, "Salem, Massachusetts."

"Oh." I looked from the letter to Richard, to

the messenger, and back to the letter again. "Oh, they're alive! They're alive!"

I hugged Richard and jumped up and down. The messenger, face flushed, nodded. Richard gave him coins from his pocket and compliments to his captain.

I could not believe it. Abby and Nate had been rescued!

"Well, Hannah," Richard's voice came to me through my delirium. "I told you I'd find them for you, didn't I?"

Chapter Thirteen

My Dear Hannah:

Where do I begin? I pray this will reach you. I am putting these words down in haste since Captain James Barr of the Suffolk told us he plans to set sail tomorrow morning, because he expects good winds. And he has promised to get this letter aboard the first ship he meets that is bound for the coast of New England.

He is such a dear man, Hannah. Without him and his crew, Nate and I would not be alive. Although there were still gale winds when he hove into view, he would not abandon us, but stood by all night and through the next morning, as his boats and men fought their way back and forth between his ship and ours not only to save us but to salvage whatever they could of our belongings and cargo.

All except one of our crew was saved. Hannah, words cannot describe the relentless storm, the boiling ocean, the waves that crashed over us, the ship's rollings and creakings and motions, the sailors, their language, and their brave behavior. No one could stand upright long and nothing could be kept in its place.

Nate had ordered all the sails down, of course, with the exception of a foresail with which he hoped to scud, but the wind tore that from bottom to top.

The noises, Hannah, were as from hell itself. The men and Nate had to scream to be heard. The shrouds and all the other ship's ropes made their own terrible howling. The ocean boiled with white and with every assault of waves, the ship groaned and wrenched with ripping and tearing sounds, like an old man in an ague.

Lightning hit the mainmast and burned a hole in the top of a seaman's head. He lived through all this for three days, Hannah, in agony, and died raving mad. I and Liddy did our best to attend him but at the end Nate had to order him tied to his hammock, which itself pitched in the storm as the ship darted from side to side. Attending him made me forget my own fear, but I fell and wrenched my shoulder.

Our real worry was that the lightning would travel to the magazine and ignite the gunpowder. But it did not. Water was tumbling into the hold and the ship's carpenters were rushing about with tools to patch the damage. The chain pumps reduced the water to three feet.

We lost some of our timbers. I think at one time we did not eat for two days. Merlin was busy helping the crew and Liddy did her best to get fresh water and emergency rations to us, fruit and leftover biscuits and salt meat.

The Suffolk hove into view on the third or fourth day. We managed to save some cargo and personal items. I have my part of the quilt, Hannah, though it is a little damp. And my journal and Cornwallis, the parrot, who screamed throughout the whole storm, "Water in the hold, water in the hold!" I think the poor dear was quite frightened. He also used some terrible seamen's language, which I cannot repeat here.

Once aboard the Suffolk, we were only a little better off, because she was taking on water, too. But her pumps solved that problem and before long we were comfortable, in seas that turned to innocent smoothness, and on our way to the Canaries.

Liddy is quite good taking care of the sick. She gave me remedies for pain from my shoulder. I did not find out until we were safely aboard the Suffolk that Nate had injuries. His ankle was badly sprained and he had been hit on the head by a large splinter of wood from the mainmast. But I think that seeing the Swamp Fox shiver violently as the sea went over her and she went under hurt him most of all. He is mending and vows to rebuild her.

We've been resting at the home of friends of

Captain Barr's. They have extended every courtesy to us. I have requested a piece of fabric from them both, as well as from Captain Barr, for my part of the quilt.

Oh, Hannah, I have thought of you so often! Nate says I am now a midshipman, at least, after what I have been through. He feels hurt sore that my first voyage ended this way. But he acquitted himself as ship's master so well, and when I realize that by his intelligence and courage, he saved our lives, I am gratified to have been a part of this voyage.

I shall write again. We shall take passage back to Charleston as soon as we can, though I do not know when that will be. Give my love to Cabot and Margaret and Mattie. Do you ever hear from Father? Does he ever ask after me? Give him my love, if you write. And convey my warmest wishes to all our friends in Salem. Hannah, I cry when I think of home, of you in your garden, of my girlhood room. My heart is full to bursting these days with gratitude to God for sparing us.

Your loving sister, Abigail.

When August came Margaret insisted upon having the party. I didn't want a party. But her eyes had filled with tears when I told her of my betrothal to Richard and I could not say no. All I could do was point out the pitfalls.

"Most of the townfolk are turned against Richard because they fear he is involved in the slave trade," I said.

"What they fear," she returned, "these great shipowners, the Elias Derbys and the Crowninshield family and all others of their ilk, is that their feudal lordship over this village is being challenged by the young upstart, Richard Lander."

I stood, stock-still. Margaret was a foreigner, a housekeeper, and she understood our town better than I.

"I never thought of that, Margaret," I said.

"And I'm sure you've never thought of this, either. His father took blame for goin' against the Continental Congress. Myself, I'm thinkin' it's more than profit that lures your Richard on a long and difficult voyage. Methinks it's by way of restorin' his family name."

I nodded, yes. That made sense, too. "But Richard doesn't mix with people, Margaret. He isn't social."

"Then mayhap it's time he started. If he expects to be a leadin' merchant in town, he'll have to be social. So this party will be by way of introducin' him. And announcin' your betrothal."

"True, but if we tell Richard that, he won't want the party."

"Then we'll tell him it's in celebration of Abby and Nate bein' found rescued. And to present the wee bairn to everyone. Don't you think it's time we did that?"

I agreed with my mouth. But in my heart I still didn't like the idea.

However, I knew it was time to start thinking about many things. Taking Night Song out of the house, for instance. Having her baptized, giving her a Christian name. We could not go on calling her Night Song or "the bairn" forever. Nor could we keep her hidden from the townfolk, like some shameful secret.

There had been enough shameful secrets in this family, I decided. I would not be like my father and germinate more.

So one fine day, the first week in August, I asked Mattie to accompany me to tea at her mother's shop, and to bring Night Song along. We dressed her in the newest little frock made by Margaret, with embroidery on the edges.

She was near three months old now and not only smiling, but making little baby noises, cooing when one spoke to her. She would lie, for hours, on a quilt in my garden and laugh at the leaves dancing overhead and throwing shadows in the sun. She was an alert and bright baby and her dark eyes had all of the stars in them.

We took tea with Mary, who had a small landing that extended out over the water in back of her shop. If I'd been at all distressed with Mary for not telling me the truth about my mother, how my father had treated her and that she'd had a dalliance with Burnaby, I could not stay angry.

She was Mary, my dear friend. And, as Richard had said, the old generation that came through the war kept many a secret locked inside them.

That afternoon the tea Mary had prepared was special, with an iced cake she had made in celebration of my betrothal to her son. She greeted me like a mother. When she put her arms around me, I felt as if I'd come home. She was making a gift, too, embroidered sheets for my dowry chest.

We had a grand time, planning and talking and fussing over the baby. It was late afternoon by the time we left. As we rushed along the wharf, intent on being home for supper, a voice called to me above the din and confusion.

"Good day, Miss Chelmsford. How fortunate to meet you like this. It saves me a trip to your house, though that is something I've little desire to be saved from."

Mr. Leonard. Mattie and I paused. He took off his hat and bowed.

"What a pleasant surprise, ladies. Miss Chelmsford, I just recently heard of your betrothal to Richard Lander."

I gasped. "How did you hear that?"

He smiled. "Indeed. I've lived here only a short time, but already I know that there are no secrets in Salem. Lander's probably told some of his crew. And they do frequent coffee and ale houses. Is it something you wanted to keep secret?"

I did not reply.

"For that I cannot blame you. After all, having

your name bandied about in connection with the master of a slave ship could have a most undesirable effect in town."

I held back a retort. To deny that the *Prince* was a slaver was to give Leonard what he wanted. He was too clever to believe such. The look in his eyes told me he knew better. But he would get no information from me.

"Ah, but then, from what I hear, it wouldn't be the first time a female member of the Chelmsford family had her name bandied about in Salem, would it?"

I wanted to strike him. Oh, the man was a viper! "To what member of my family do you refer, Mr. Leonard?" I asked innocently.

His smile was sly and cunning. "Why, your sister Abby, of course. Eloping as she did. People did talk. Is there any other female member of your family whose name has been bandied about carelessly?"

He was speaking of my mother. But he didn't dare say it. I felt sick. "Really, Mr. Leonard, we are late for supper. We must go."

But he deliberately blocked our way. Now his evil glance rested on the baby in Mattie's arms. "So, this is the child everyone is talking about." He reached out as if to touch Night Song. Instinctively, Mattie pulled back.

"*Who* is talking about her, Mr. Leonard?" I demanded.

"Why just about everyone in town."

I drew myself up. "And does everyone in town know that she is the daughter of Louis Gaudineer who is serving under Captain Finney of the Pennsylvania Militia? And who has been risking his life to protect our settlers?"

"I don't know about that, Miss Hannah," he said cheerfully, "but they do know she is half-Indian. And I know that sentiment for the American savage does not run favorably in this town amongst families of those who have gone west. Especially *now*."

Something in the way he said *now* bestirred me. "Why now?" I asked. "What has happened?"

His smile this time was slow and insidious. "Dear child, don't you read the paper?" And from under his arm he took a folded copy of the *Salem Mercury*.

" 'Kentuckians,' " he read slowly and carefully, " 'have ridden north and laid waste to some Shawnee towns.' " He looked at me. "According to this report, about eight hundred Kentucky horsemen have burned thirteen Shawnee villages, killing many warriors and women and children."

I drew in my breath. Louis had feared such an attack from the Kentuckians.

"From what I hear at the Sun Tavern," Mr. Leonard went on, "the Kentuckians attacked in retaliation for Indian raids along the Ohio. Now the peace is shaken. And settlers fear the Indians will strike back."

I felt my face go white, my knees buckle.

"So you can understand, Miss Hannah, why people aren't going to take kindly to you having a half-Indian child in your house."

"She's a *baby*. Her own mother was killed by Kentuckians."

"People aren't likely to care about that, especially if the Indians start attacking their families out there."

I closed my eyes for a second to get my bearings. When I did, I spoke plain. "What is it you want from me, Mr. Leonard?"

"Want? Nothing, Miss Hannah. I promised your father I'd look in on you while he's away."

"I need no protection from you," I said.

"Come now. You are under suspicion since your betrothal to Lander. Remember, his vessel has been attacked in the harbor. People know he frequents your home. Now you have this child, another target for people's wrath. I could find a home for her, take her off your hands. There's a woman at the mill who's recently lost a child and is in mourning. She would gladly take the little one in."

"*A woman at the mill!*" I could not believe it. "Mr. Leonard, this is a friend's child. I am taking care of her for him. She is my responsibility, and no one else's."

He shook his head, sadly. "You'd do well to heed my words. Your father has worked hard to restore his reputation, after that unpleasantness with your mother and my people during the war.

He won't look favorably on your betrothal to Lander. He'll look less favorably on your taking in a half-Indian baby."

"If my father is not in favor of my actions, Mr. Leonard, I will answer to him," I said.

He bowed. "Very well, Miss Hannah. May I offer you some advice just the same?"

I sighed. "You may. I can see there is no way for me to avoid listening."

"Pay some mind to the girls at the mill," he said. "This mill means a lot to your father. Your taking an interest in it will soften his heart toward you despite your other actions."

"I'm not trying to soften his heart."

"Perhaps you should be. But if not for that reason, then for the girls. They are badly in need of female supervision. You might pay them a visit. Before the old biddies in town do."

"The old biddies?"

"Yes. I speak of Mrs. Haffield White and company. They are speaking of inspecting the premises."

"Would that be so bad?"

"You know what troublemakers they are, Miss Hannah. If they knew you were taking charge of the girls, they would leave us alone."

I took a deep breath. "I can wish you no better fate than a visit by Mrs. White and company, Mr. Leonard," I said. "Come, Mattie, it's late."

As we walked away, he called after me. "You know how much this mill means to your father,

Miss Hannah. I know you don't like me. But I can be of help to you when he comes home."

At least I think that's what he said. What with the confusion and noise on the wharves, I couldn't be sure.

Chapter Fourteen

When I got home two letters from Lawrence were waiting. One was for Mattie, the other for me. I took mine out to the privacy of my garden to sit with a cup of tea and read.

Dear Hannah: I write to you from the town of Maysville in Kentucky Territory. Father didn't stay around long in Marietta. The first week there he met with three land speculators and decided to go into partnership with them.

They plan a great port city directly across the Ohio from the mouth of the Licking River. It is northwest of Maysville. I tried talking Father into staying in Marietta, but a trading post had already been established there. We will stay here for another week, then set out to the new site.

Father will leave Thankful here with some fine people we have met. She'll have some schooling. She does not want to stay. I have suggested we bring her along and not make others responsible for her, but he refuses to listen.

Settlements are coming to life all over Kentucky. I met Simon Kenton, a frontiersman. He has a station on the south shore of the Ohio, and a two-story brick house on Lawrence Creek. He was gracious enough to extend us hospitality for two nights. He knows Daniel Boone and George Rogers Clark. And the Shawnee chief, Blue Jacket, who was a white youngster of seventeen when he went off to live as an Indian back in '71.

Mr. Kenton meets all the emigrants who land at the mouth of the Limestone Creek. He looks like an Indian, except for his blue eyes. He has allowed me to sketch him.

Don't be concerned, Hannah. I know you people back east hear many stories about Indian attacks. But Simon Kenton is a great frontiersman and well-known protector of the settler. He and his volunteers are all over, guarding the lives and property of hundreds of families. They chase attacking Indians, recover stolen property, and there is a great feeling of well-being, knowing they are here.

I hope you and Cabot are well. Do you hear from Abby and Nate? How often I recollect that night of the party. I know Abby is happy and we did right helping her.

Yes, we have seen Indians, but only from a

distance. I hope someday to sit in on a treaty and perhaps get to sketch them. You may write to me here at Maysville. I enclose the address. It will get forwarded to me sooner or later.

Keep well and give my love to Cabot. Yr. affectionate brother, Lawrence.

Our party was to be a good old-fashioned bean supper. Plain food. Richard had requested that. Margaret agreed. After all, Richard was sailing in two weeks.

I did not want to contemplate that. So I kept busy. I directed John Gardener, Cabot, and Richard as they set up trestle tables in the brick court-yard behind the house. It joined my garden, which was in full bloom. Lanterns were strung over-head.

My roses, red and white, scented the air. My row of current bushes were in good order. The corner of vegetables, my summer squash and cucumbers and tomatoes, were promising a good harvest. Under my pear tree in a far corner was my hen coop, housing at least six hens and George the Third, the rooster.

Mattie put fresh flower petals in the little pond that Lawrence had made. It was fed from a natural spring. My hop vine clambered over the arbor at the gate, and Mattie and I festooned the long tables with garlands of fern. Then we cut fresh flowers to put in the cut glass bowls that served as centerpieces.

It was when we were finishing up, early in the afternoon, that I noticed the man watching us from across the street.

He was half-hidden behind some bushes. The first time I saw him, he ducked completely behind the bushes. The second time, he stepped out, boldly, stared directly at me, and then walked away.

My heart seemed to thump inside me. I did not know the man and I know most everyone in Salem. Was he a stranger, off a ship? One of Richard's crew, keeping watch for some reason? I said nothing to anyone and then in the hustle and bustle of the next few hours I forgot him completely.

I knew how many people I had invited to the party and so I sensed, early on, that we were being rebuffed. Within the first hour only a dozen souls came through our garden gate. And the sight of the empty tables mocked me.

Reverend Bentley came, of course. And Mary Gardener, with four of her children. Richard's mother brought friends. And so did Mattie. Some of Richard's crew had been invited, but they kept to themselves at a table near my garden.

None of the women whose menfolk had gone west came. And I'd invited them all. Mrs. Haffield White, Mrs. Cooper, and Mrs. Moulton did not come. Neither did any of the others who had come to the farewell party for Father.

"Margaret, where is everyone? Who will eat all this food?"

She and the girls she had hired were bringing heaping platters and tureens of food out to the tables. Fish chowder, little partridges in jellied stock, creamed scallops, lobster, salmon, and English mutton. Clam pie and blueberry buckle, as well as Margaret's pickled preserves, steaming hot breads, cider, and wine. Margaret's version of a simple bean supper.

"Everyone who cares about you is here," was all she would say. She was stirring some lobsters in a pot, set up on a tripod over a fire.

"The people I invited haven't come!" I was near tears. I felt sick inside. I wanted to run into the house and jump into bed and cover my head with my quilt.

"It's their loss then, isn't it?" she asked.

"Margaret, you don't understand." I looked about me wildly. "When people don't come to a party, it's an insult! It's a disgrace."

"On them who are rude enough to do such a thing," she said.

"Margaret, I'm going inside. I'm won't stay out here and be humiliated!"

"You can only be humiliated if you permit yourself to be," she said.

She made maddening sense, as always. But I still wanted to cry.

"You draw these people close to you this night, child. If you leave now, it's them who will be insulted. And why should such be? They've come to honor you. They bring gifts. Stand next to Richard, accept their good wishes and their gifts, and know that many have started out a betrothal with less. And count your blessings."

Over the steam of the lobster pot, I stared at her.

"If you let those who did not come ruin this night, they have won." Her face was red, gray hair tumbled out of her mobcap, which was askew on her head. But she uttered her words from the depth of her soul. So I knew them to be true. Truer than any parson's words from the pulpit.

"Thank you, Margaret," I said. And so I settled down a bit and went to greet our guests.

Parson Bentley gave the blessing before we ate. ". . . upon Hannah. And Richard, who, as the old song from the War of Independence put it, 'goes 't'other side of the wave,' " he intoned. And everyone bowed their heads as he went on.

I did not bow my head. I cast an eye on little Night Song, asleep in her cradle. Then, from the corner of my eye I saw the men across the street, watching us. And I knew in that moment that we were in trouble.

Men assembled in Salem for all kinds of reasons. To see a ship come in. Or to watch one clear the harbor. Sometimes they assembled in front of somebody's house if news came that a father or brother was lost at sea.

The militia assembled for parades. But I knew

in an instant that this assembly was an unsavory group, up to no good.

At first they just stood there. Then they came a little into the street. No one noticed. Parson Bentley finished his prayer and a toast was drunk.

"Let's commence dancing," someone said.

The hired musicians had not shown up, either.

"Just from the smell of the clam pie, I can tell you it's their loss," said the parson. "But there are a few gentlemen who have brought musical instruments. I can think of nothing more fitting than dancing to songs of the sea."

"Them's the kinda dances they do on a slaver, Parson?" The voice came through the dusk as one man walked up to our garden gate.

Two members of Richard's crew had just started to play their jaunty music. As the question was flung across the gate, like a gauntlet thrown down, the music stopped. Everyone looked at the approaching men. Richard came to stand beside me.

"May I be of some help to you gentlemen?" the parson asked.

"You know what we want." A disembodied voice floated in the night air. "We want to give notice to Miss Chelmsford. We don't take to no Indians in Salem."

"There are no Indians here," Richard said.

"What about that little papoose?"

"She is the daughter of a Pennsylvania militiaman, who at this moment is rounding up more men in Connecticut and New Jersey, to take back to the frontier to help defend our settlers," Richard told them.

"That's a half-Indian baby." An accusing voice came out of the crowd.

"Yes," Richard answered. "And the reason she is here is because her father had nowhere else to leave her. Her mother was killed by Kentuckians. White men who raided a Shawnee village when the warriors were away. And who put a hatchet in her mother's skull while the woman fled with the child in her arms."

Silence, so terrible I could hear the beating of my heart. And the chirping of the night bugs.

"You expect us to believe that story?" one of the men asked. "From you, who lie to us about ownin' a slave ship?"

"I've lied to no one," Richard said. "What rumors have circulated about my mission, you have started on your own. I know you men. I saw you at the wharf. The night my vessel was struck with mud and rocks and eggs."

"Too bad it weren't gunpowder," a voice said. "Still could be, Lander. People hereabouts don't take to a slaver any more than to an Indian."

Richard stepped forward. For a moment he surveyed the crowd. "In whose name do you come?" he asked.

"The good people of Salem," came the answer.

"The good people of Salem can say what they wish about me," Richard's voice rang out. "I've never concerned myself before and I'm not about to start concerning myself now. But I do care that you interrupt these my friends at their gathering, that you upset Miss Chelmsford and malign an innocent babe."

Mumblings from the crowd.

"Take your anger out on someone who can defend himself," Richard said. "Or do the men of Salem now pick on the defenseless?"

No answer.

"I shall gladly come out into the street if you wish. But I should advise you that I have some of my crew here. I would say the odds are about even."

While he spoke, his men came forward. I saw no pistols, but their very presence indicated that in a second they would come to Richard's defense if need be.

"The rest of my men are back at the wharf, guarding my ship. Now, make your decision. Do we come out into the street?"

More murmurings from the men, but no one accepted the invitation.

"Exactly as I thought," Richard said. "And I put it to you that you do not represent the citizens of Salem. Admit it. I don't know who you represented the night you attacked my ship but I'll wager that tonight you represent Mr. Leonard, who is chagrined because he has not been able to make progress in his romantic advances to Miss Chelmsford."

"We don't know no Mr. Leonard," one of the voices said.

"Then why don't you look around behind you," Richard suggested. "He's standing across the street there in the shadows, watching."

Some of the men turned. Others didn't bother. Then Richard did something that I shall remember as long as I live.

Without so much as a glance at me, he walked to the cradle and picked up Night Song. I watched him handle her gingerly and held my breath. *What was he doing?* He had never so much as given the child a second glance before this.

Carefully, he nestled her in his arms. Softly he spoke to her. She had just come awake. The child never cried upon waking, but would look around and gurgle in contentment. Now she smiled up at Richard as he spoke to her tenderly.

Then he started walking across the lawn to the gate and the men assembled in the street.

"Richard!" I said in a loud whisper. But Parson Bentley put a restraining hand on my arm.

With his free hand, Richard opened the gate and stepped into the street. He walked into the midst of the men. The silence made the moment stand out like a drop in time. No one moved. Some of the men held pine torches and they illuminated the scene with an eerie light.

Others moved aside as Richard came into their midst, like waters parting for Moses.

Cradling the child carefully, Richard looked around him, peering into the faces of the men. "This is Night Song," he said. "That's her Shawnee name. Miss Chelmsford has yet to pick a Christian name for her. But one will be given, when she is christened."

Several of the men backed away.

Richard went up to one of the older ones, who appeared to be, in manner of dress at least, less of a threat than the others.

"I know you, Mr. Atwater," Richard said. "See you at the wharves all the time. You're an investor in one of Mr. Derby's East Indiamen, aren't you?"

The man nodded, shamefacedly.

"You've grandchildren, as I hear it." And Richard thrust the baby toward him. "Take her," he urged, "go ahead, you've grandchildren. You know how to hold them."

I felt myself gasp and go faint. Parson Bentley steadied me.

In the eeriness of the torchlight I saw Mr. Atwater accept Night Song, hold her like a basket of eggs, and stand rigid.

She cooed up at him. She waved a small fist.

"That's quite a smile, isn't it?" Richard asked. "And look at those bright eyes. She takes notice of everything. Right smart, she is."

Some of the men stepped forward to look at the baby. On the edges of the light, I saw Richard's men encircling, unnoticed, around the crowd in the street. And I breathed easier.

"Miss Chelmsford was thinking of naming her Georgianna," Richard told them. "In honor of George Washington. What do you think, Mr. Atwater? Do you think it's fitting?"

The man nodded yes, and gave the baby back.

Richard looked around him. "Anybody else want her? Here's your chance. You want to take her out of this house? Take her. Here and now."

It was a challenge. And it stunned them as much as it stunned me. Again there was that terrible silence. And the night bugs' song seemed raised to a pitch.

"Take her now," Richard said quietly, "or hereafter leave her in peace. Who wants this child? This half-Indian child. Who wants to harm her?"

The men grumbled. There was a shuffling of feet. I heard one of them accuse another, a retort in self-defense. Then someone said, "Let's go home. Let's get out of here. There's no profit in this."

"We men of Salem don't do harm to babies," someone else said.

And they dispersed into the night. As quickly as they had come. Richard stood there in the street, surrounded by his men, until they were all gone. Then he turned.

By now all of us were at the gate. Tears were streaming down my face. Richard walked back to the gate and handed Night Song to me over it.

"Here's your baby, Hannah," he said. "They won't bother you about her anymore."

"Oh, Richard!" I hugged the child to me and Richard kissed me over the gate. A cheer went up from his men. They gave three "huzzahs," the old Revolutionary War cheer and threw their hats up into the air.

And then the party began.

Chapter Fifteen

The *Prince* was supposed to clear Salem Harbor on the last day of August. She was ready. I'd gone with Richard to fill out the registry certificate, seen it signed by Joseph Hiller, the custom's officer in charge of the port of Salem.

She was registered as being 150 tons. Her crew was ten. She was armed with two guns. The certificate stated that she was built in Salem in 1774, owner Nathaniel Chelmsford, that she had been outfitted to be a privateer in 1775 and rebuilt in 1788 to be a three-masted square rigger, present master Richard Lander.

The certificate listed her destination as India. Her cargo was two pipes of brandy, fifty-eight cases of gin, twelve tons of iron, two hogsheads of tobacco, and two boxes of salmon.

On the afternoon of the twenty-eighth, a note came from Richard. He couldn't come to supper, he would send Cabot home at dusk. But when darkness fell there was still no Cabot. I wasn't worried. Cabot had been helping Richard almost every day after school for the past week.

I had just seated myself at the dining room table, alone, to take my meal. Mattie came rushing in.

"Richard asked if you could come to the wharf."

I looked up. She seemed to be an apparition. Her hair tumbled rudely to her shoulders, her face was red with cold for the evening had turned chill. I knew something was wrong.

"What is it?"

"He's clearing the harbor tonight."

"Does that mean he dinna come for supper?" Margaret appeared in the door of the dining room, a steaming platter in her hands. "I've made scallops just the way he likes them!"

Richard had come for supper almost every night since the party, sometimes late, but he came. Margaret spoiled him, fussing over him and making all his favorite foods, never complaining when she had to keep supper warm because of his tardiness.

"Tonight?" I croaked. My hand flew to my throat. "No, he sails in three days, Mattie."

"Tonight," she insisted. And I saw my own fear reflected in her eyes. "Cabot was delivering a message for him in the Sun Tavern and heard talk that someone has organized a new mob. Ropewalk workers! Give them liquor and they'll form a mob in an instant. They plan to pay the *Prince* another visit tomorrow. This time with gunpowder. Richard means to slip out under cover of darkness within the hour."

Within the hour. The words sounded a knell in my bones. My world came crashing down. *Richard was leaving tonight.*

"He's got the wind and tide," Mattie said.

I got up. Margaret was next to me, holding my cloak. She slipped it around my shoulders, while I stood woodenly. Then she patted me on the face. "I'll put the creamed scallops in a covered dish," she said.

"There isn't time," Mattie called after her as she went into the kitchen.

"He'll be gone a year," Margaret called back. "He can wait five minutes for my creamed scallops."

I stood on the quarterdeck of the *Prince* with Mattie, each of us hugging our cloaks close. There was a wind and it was blowing out to sea. My head swirled. Richard had greeted me with a quick kiss on the cheek and bade us go to his cabin. But we stood fast, I holding the covered dish of scallops.

I barely had a minute with him, he was so busy. He held a ledger in hand, giving orders to his first mate, Mr. Corbett. "Is the powder secured?" he asked.

"It is, sir, and the rest of the arms will be here in a minute."

The last of Richard's men were coming aboard, just rounded up from various ordinaries in town. The latecomers lugged their sea chests and canvas bags. But Richard seemed to be waiting anxiously for someone special.

All was a confusion of sights and sounds, embedded forever in my senses, forms coming out of the darkness, whispered conversations, lanterns casting larger-than-life shadows, the lapping of the water at the sides of the ship, the creaking of winches, Richard's voice, subdued but authoritative.

The activity was much the same as the afternoon of the maiden voyage, only now there was an undertone of finality to it. I felt things ending. And there was nothing I could do about it. I stood about, helplessly.

By the light of the lanterns, I watched his face as he questioned his first and second mates, and gave orders to his carpenter and clerk about last-minute matters. He was sharp and smart, to use his own words. But I felt as if I were in a nightmare.

Richard was leaving. But it was too soon. We still had two whole days! I'd planned supper on the *Prince* in two nights. Mattie was to help me make it. Now there would be no night-before-sailing supper. Tonight he'd clear the channel and be out at sea.

I minded a wrenching and tearing inside me. This was farewell. I was plunging into that dark hole inside me. Tears started gathering in my eyes. I must becalm myself. This night was the coming together of all Richard's work and planning. I must not muddle it up for him.

Then in the next moment something caught my eye. Cabot was coming up the gangway, saying something to Richard, who was nodding and smiling.

Then a wagon drew up on the wharf and some men lifted a large chest from it and carried it aboard. Richard gave Cabot an order and my brother ran past me.

"Cabot. What are you about?"

He was dirty and excited. And greatly pleased with himself. "Helping." He paused for just a second to look up at me. "I found out they're planning to attack the *Prince*, Hannah. I told Richard. He said I may have saved her. And I just fetched the man who's supplying the firearms. I must go now. Show them where to stow the firearms below deck."

Firearms! Sure enough, that's what was in the chest. Muskets. The men marched past me with the chest, following Cabot.

I turned to Mattie. "What are they for?"

She shrugged. "Wherever Richard's going, he may need them," she said simply.

At that moment another wagon drew up on the wharf and I recognized Mary Lander with some men. She alighted and started directing them to carry some barrels aboard.

"It's Mama with the fruit," Mattie said. She crossed the quarterdeck and I followed.

"Fruit?"

"Yes." Mattie flung me a smile. "Apples, pears,

lemons, limes, berries. And fresh vegetables. Everything Mama could lay her hands on. Richard is determined to keep his men healthy." She took my hand and peered into my face. "Don't look so worried, Hannah. Richard knows what he's about."

"Why does he have such a crew, Mattie? And so many guns? He's registered ten men and two guns. I saw the certificate."

She smiled. "He's also registered his destination as India, hasn't he? He's got eight guns and fifteen men. More men than a trans-Atlantic schooner and less than an East Indiaman. Come on, we'll go to the galley and ask the cook if we can make coffee. I'm sure Mama's brought some cakes. And we'll reheat those creamed scallops."

Richard gave his mother a long embrace, kissed his sister, and stood for a moment, watching them go up the companionway with Cabot. Then he closed the door of the captain's cabin and looked at me.

"Tell Margaret I enjoyed the creamed scallops," he said.

I was securing the last of the coffee cups in a cupboard. We had all had coffee and cake while Richard ate the scallops. "She wanted to make sure you didn't miss out on them," I said awkwardly.

"I'm sorry you didn't get to give your farewell party."

"Yes, but at least we all enjoyed your mother's cake."

In the next moment we were in each other's arms. I clung to him. "I want to be a good captain's wife, Richard," I said, "though we're not married yet. I want to send you off the right way. But I don't know the right way."

He kissed me, a long and tender kiss. "You're doing everything right. But there is one thing."

I drew back. "What?"

He held my hands in his own. "You've been so good about not asking my destination. I would tell you now, Hannah, where I'm going."

"No," I said quickly.

"No?" He was disbelieving. "Why?"

"I want to know, yes, Richard. But I want, more, for you to know I trust you."

His blue eyes darkened with feeling and he held me close. I could feel the beating of his heart.

"Let that trust be a farewell gift from me to you," I said. "I was having a gift made for you, a beautifully bound journal for you to write in. But I was to pick it up tomorrow."

"I was having some scrimshaw made for you. A necklace. It was to be finished in two days," he said.

We both laughed. Then I remembered something. "I want something else from you," I said.

"Name it, Hannah."

"A piece of fabric from something you wear. For my quilt."

There was a brief tap on the door then. "All's ready, sir."

"Aye," Richard said. He looked around the cabin. "Everything's stowed and secured. Hannah, I've nothing."

Our eyes met. Then Richard moved toward his desk, unlocked a drawer, took out a knife, and in one swift movement removed his coat, pulled his shirttail out of his trousers, and began slashing away at the white fabric.

In a moment he had a decent white square of good cotton. Then he undid the black silk stock at his neck. "This is all I have to give you, Hannah," he said.

I clutched the piece of fabric and the silk stock in my hand. Tears came to my eyes. "Oh, Richard, you have given me so much more."

He raised his hands, palms upward, in a gesture of despair. "What have I given you, Hannah? I can't even marry you before I sail, because I've nothing to offer."

"Nothing? Richard, you have given me so much! What you did at the party with baby Night Song, I shall never forget. You have ensured her safety in Salem. You had ships' masters all over the ocean looking for Abby and Nate. You brought Cabot back to me. And if I hadn't met Burnaby I would never have settled things in my mind about my mother."

"I did all that?" he asked in mock surprise.

"Yes. But most of all you gave me my trust, Richard."

He looked down at me in such a way that I have never been looked at by a man. All the world was in his eyes. And I knew, as I heard whistles shrieking above us, heard men shouting and footsteps scurrying, that I would have to keep that look in my heart for a year. It would be all I would have to remember him by.

Chapter Sixteen

It rained for a week after Richard left. I was quite beside myself. There is nothing worse than rain in early September. The house seemed to be bathed in a half-light all day and when I looked out at my flower garden it seemed as if it would never survive the downpour.

A chill fell over everything and we lit fires in the hearth. Cabot was restless when he wasn't in school. He insisted upon going out. He would dress in oilskins that Richard had given him and haunt his familiar places at the wharves. But it was different now. He came home on time. And after supper he holed up in his room and studied the many books Richard had given him on naval architecture, preferring them to his schoolwork.

Night Song, as we still called the baby, kept us all sane. She was growing right before our eyes. Her face became even rounder and she filled the house with her baby cooing and gurgling.

I knew that at some time I must christen this child. Margaret kept asking me about it, saying she was "heathen" and we must give her a proper name. But I was waiting.

I did not know what for. It was as if I were waiting for something to happen. I went back to my quilting. But it was a heart-wrenching job, because Abigail's and Thankful's parts of the quilt were missing. And I felt too many parts of me missing, also. Afternoons, that week after Richard left I would sit in the back parlor at the quilt frame all alone and watch the rain pouring against the windows, watch the candles flicker, and think of Richard. I put the white fabric he had given me in a special square in the quilt and trimmed it with the black silk from his stock. I missed Richard so! Impossible to believe he was gone. And every day, when Cabot returned from the school or the wharves, he would wander in and sit with me as I quilted. We would make conversation. He would tell me what was going on at the wharves, what ships were in, what captains were loading cargo. But it was a desultory conversation, with spaces in it. Just like my quilt. And I knew Cabot missed Richard, too. But I could not help him.

The rain stopped at the end of the week, finally, and a September sun bathed us in its warmth. I had always loved September. I ventured out into my garden to see what damage the storms had wrought. The world was sun-washed and bright as a newly minted coin. I was standing there in the middle of the garden, smelling the harbor waters, wondering where the *Prince* was now.

"Hannah."

I looked up. Louis stood there, just outside the garden gate, holding his horse's reins. He was wearing his frontier clothing and he was very sun-bronzed.

"I've recruited two hundred and fifty men from New Jersey, Pennsylvania, and Connecticut," he said. "They're stationed here, in Massachusetts, at Springfield. We march in a week. Hannah, I must talk with you."

In the pristine white dining room, with the Persian carpet and the delicate white curtains and wallpaper printed with English hunting scenes, Louis seemed so primitive. His clothing bespoke another way of life.

Margaret had brought in bread and meat and I poured coffee out of my mother's silver pot, which had been made by Paul Revere.

"Sit and eat," I said, "you look starved."

He ate, ravenously. "There's trouble brewing on the frontier," he said.

"We heard about the Kentuckians."

He nodded. "The peace has been severely shaken. The government is demanding aggressive action. Henry Knox, Secretary of War, knows we can't crush the Indians. We haven't the army. He wants to treat with them, instead. But others will insist on using military force."

I watched him eating. It seemed so unseemly to

speak of such things in that room with the Hepplewhite table and sideboard, the gentle September breeze lifting the fragile curtains and bringing in the fragrance of garden flowers.

"I'm afraid of trouble on the frontier, Louis," I said.

He nodded and sipped his coffee. A clock ticked decorously on the mantle, marking the measured, gentle hours in the house.

Across the polished table, Louis looked at me with those blue eyes of his. "I can't take the baby back with me, Hannah," he said. "And I've been to see my folks in Philadelphia. They don't want her."

I just stared at him. "How can they not want her? She's their grandchild."

"It's as I've suspected. Because she's half-Indian."

I nodded as if I understood, as if that explained everything. But I did not understand. "Your mother and father, as I remember them, were so . . . kind, Louis, so civilized."

"Exactly," he agreed. "Can you fancy them taking in a baby who is half-Indian? My father is a merchant. My mother has all her proper friends. Perhaps they are *too* civilized.

"They asked me to make other arrangements. They suggested I take her back to her mother's people. My father put forth the theory that it would not be kind to force the child to grow up in Philadelphia. He said she would never be happy and he couldn't allow himself or another to be responsible for her unhappiness."

"How can parents be so heartless?" I asked. And then I was sorry I said it, for Louis just gave me a long and beseeching look across the table. "*You* have to ask that, Hannah?"

"No," I murmured. "I'm sorry, Louis. What will you do with her, then?"

"I was hoping you would take her."

"Take her?"

"Yes. Keep her for me. Bring her up, until I return from the frontier."

I had to clear my throat to speak. My voice cracked. There was a roaring in my ears. "How long will that be, Louis?"

"I don't know," he said gravely, "perhaps years. Perhaps never. I could get killed out there, Hannah, defending the settlers. It would help knowing, if that happened, that my child was in good hands."

I could not think. My lips were dry. *Raise the baby!* It was one thing keeping her for two months, but quite another agreeing to keep her for a lifetime. I could not answer.

"I know it's a lot to ask of you, Hannah," he said, "but I don't know what else to do, whom else to turn to. I can't take her back with me. What else can I do?" He ran his hand over his eyes and slumped in his chair. "You don't have to answer now. Think on it," he said.

"When do I have to answer?"

He looked around the dining room as if solutions were to be found in its quiet corners, in the sunlight streaming in on the polished floorboards, in the measured ticking of the clock. "I have some business to attend to here in Salem. And I'd like to visit with my daughter. If you could let me know at the end of the week, Hannah, I'd be much obliged. I'll be staying at the Blue Anchor Inn."

Louis stayed at the Blue Anchor but came every day to see his daughter. Margaret and Mattie fussed shamelessly over him, making him special foods to eat, providing him with coffee and fresh-baked goodies whenever he came in.

Cabot took Louis to the wharves, after school, and Louis allowed the boy to accompany him on business. Every day Louis would spend two hours or so with his little daughter. They would sit in the sunshine in my garden. And I would sit in the back parlor, leaving them to themselves, to visit and become acquainted. I would stand at the windows and watch Louis with the child. He was delighted with her. He played with her, amused her, talked with her in a way that was most touching.

Although he took supper with us at night, we did not speak of the child. And Louis did not push me as to what I was thinking. Indeed, if I pushed myself, I could not have said what I was thinking.

I tossed and turned at night. I walked the floors.

I stared into the flood of moonlight coming in my window. I heard the mournful cry of the sea gulls, mornings, before the house was awake. I visited the baby in the nursery, which we'd made in Thankful's room, and stared at her in her cradle.

I walked to the wharves by myself in the early morning and stood staring at the place where the *Prince* had been docked. I looked out to sea, as if to find the answer in its twinkling endlessness. Somewhere out there was Richard. What would he say about my agreeing to raise Louis's baby?

I went to see Mary in her shop. We sat over tea. "You want to keep the child, don't you?" she asked.

"I don't know, Mary. What of Richard? It isn't right to make the decision when he's away. Then I think of the child. And how she has no place in the world."

"Like Cabot?" Mary asked.

I stared at her, marveling at her ability to understand so well. "Yes, like Cabot. But suppose, like my father never accepted Cabot, Richard never accepts the child."

"You must make this decision yourself," Mary said. "You know Richard, by now, better than I."

"Why won't you help me, Mary?"

"Because it is something only you can decide."

"How?"

"Look in your heart. What's there?"

"What's there is trying to keep my family together. Trying to heal the rift in my family. It seems like all my life, I've been trying to make sense of it, to piece it all together."

"Like the quilt?" Mary asked.

"Yes, like the quilt. You know, if I did it, Mary, if I raised the child, it would be Cabot all over again. It would be one more try at making it right for someone who has no place in the world."

We looked at each other. From outside came the noise and rumblings and shouting on the wharf, the crying of the sea gulls. But inside, I could hear the beating of my heart.

"You must be careful then," Mary said, "that you don't do it just to prove something. That you don't do it just to try to make right with this child what never was right with Cabot."

"But isn't that the whole point?" I asked.

"It would depend," Mary said, "on how you do it."

"Yes, I understand," I said. "I mustn't force her on anyone. I mustn't use her as a pawn to make right what never was."

"Exactly," Mary said.

"But can it be done right, then, Mary? Can I do it without making her a pawn?"

She sighed. "All of us make pawns of each other at one time or another. All of us use each other for our own purposes. But we quickly learn how that doesn't work and make amends. I would say yes, it could be done right. You will make mistakes. You sometimes will make her a pawn. But if you put your heart into it, you will end up doing it right, yes."

I thought of baby Night Song, with her bright, smiling eyes, the wide smile she gave me, upon waking, recognizing me as an old friend. I felt a tug in my heart.

"The question, Mary," I said, "is not, could I put my heart into raising her. The question is, how could I give her up?"

"It seems to me then," she allowed, "that you know what you're about to do."

I kissed her and left the shop. I went back home. I will do this thing, I told myself. For myself. And for my mother. I will make right what never was. I will tell Louis, yes, I will raise the child. I felt a soaring of spirit, walking home. I was making the right decision. I was sure of it.

I stood looking out the dining room window, watching Louis who was in the garden with Night Song. She was lying on a quilt on the soft grass, under a tree, and the two of them were bathed in the mellow light of the September afternoon, a light that already had the dappled presence of early shadows.

Soon it would be deep autumn. Louis would be gone out west. The child would remain here. I turned from the window to see his musket and blankets and rough clothing bundled up, waiting for him in the hallway.

After a while the wet nurse came into the garden. He handed the child over and came in through the back door. I heard his footsteps in the kitchen. Then he came into the dining room, where I sat, taking tea at the table.

"Where is Cabot? I'd hoped to say goodbye."

"He's at school."

He nodded. "I'd forgotten. You will give him my farewells, won't you?"

"Yes. Would you like some tea before you go?"

He came into the room, uncertainly, aware of how unseemly he looked in the delicate surroundings. I noticed how quiet his footfalls were in the moccasins. He is already walking and acting as if he is in Indian country, I told myself.

He took tea. There were some breads and meat. It was in that hour between the noon meal and supper, but he was leaving now and it did my heart good to see him eat. I knew Margaret had supplied him with her version of some good New England Muster Day gingerbread and cheese and that he carried his own supplies of food with him. Just as I knew he would rendezvous with his recruits at Springfield.

There was silence between us for a moment. Like we were wrapped in fog. Finally, he spoke.

"I can't thank you enough, Hannah. For keeping the child."

I could not trust myself to meet his eyes, at first. Because there was a note in his voice that I recognized. It was heavy with feeling and I knew the look in his eyes would match it, and I would be reminded of the old days, when we were courting and making plans.

"I shall be glad to have her, Louis. She'll make a bright spot in my life. Cabot is growing up, as you know. She is a beautiful baby."

"Yes, she is that."

"I was thinking of christening her Georgianna. Unless you have any objections. Or preferences."

"No. That would be fine."

"No final instructions as to her upbringing?"

"No. Just make her turn out like you, Hannah."

I could scarcely speak for a moment. Finally I managed. "I'll write to you and tell you how she is faring."

"That is more than I could hope for. I shall send you money. I want to bear the expenses of her upbringing."

"You've given me money enough for that, already."

"No, there will be more. It may be slow in coming, because of the mails. But I shall send it. Is there anything else I can do?"

"Yes. You can give me a piece of fabric for my quilt. Something of yours."

I did look at him then and it was exactly as I feared. The look in his eyes near tore my heart out. "I'll give you a piece of my frock coat before I leave. But it's only rough homespun."

"It's just what I want," I said.

Somehow we got through the next ten minutes without making fools of ourselves, without saying whatever it was that was bursting inside our hearts. Too late for that, we both knew. Not only too late but disastrous. It would do no good to speak of mistakes made, feelings understood too late. Besides, we were both old enough by now to understand that we might always love each other but that our lives had taken different paths and any love we might feel had not a single thing to do with those lives. Or with common sense.

When he set down his cup, he went into the hall and, with his hunting knife, cut a piece of homespun from his frock coat and gave it to me. I clutched it in my hand as he packed his belongings on his horse. I stood watching at the back door. Finished, he came to stand beside me. "I don't know how to say goodbye," he said.

"Nobody ever does, Louis."

"Surely you know, Hannah, what you are to me."

"Don't. It isn't necessary."

"For me it is. You were the dream of my youth. I loved you, Hannah. But I grew up and realized you were something I had to earn. The earning made me different. When you said no to coming west, I don't think I was surprised. I had no right to ask such from someone like you. But I'll always remember being young and loving you."

I wanted to cry then. I, the dream of his youth?

If that was true then he, in turn, was mine. But that youth was gone now. Looking up into his eyes I saw he understood this, as much as I.

"Oh, Louis!" I said. "What has life done to us?"

He smiled wryly. "Taken us by the scruff of the neck and shaken us," he said, "preyed upon us, like a wolf preys on a rabbit. We're in its grip, Hannah. We have to make the best of it, like everyone else."

I nodded, mutely.

He hugged me then and kissed me on the forehead, as a brother, as Lawrence would do. And I stood there with the piece of rough homespun in my hand and watched him mount his horse and ride away. My heart was full to bursting. I knew I might never see him again. But I also knew that the child sleeping inside in the cradle bound him to me across the years. I did not know how I felt about that. I did not know how I felt about anything, turning and going back into the house.

Everyone leaves me, I thought. Why is it my role to stand here, always, and wave goodbye? Abby and Nate, my family gone west, Richard, and now Louis. Would it soon be Cabot? I set the rough piece of homespun down on the kitchen table and tried to picture how it would look in my quilt.

Chapter Seventeen

Within a week it seemed as if everyone in Salem knew that Louis had come and gone and that I still had the baby. No one said anything about it to me, however. No one except Mrs. Haffield White.

"So you're going to keep the child." She stood there in the street and the feathers on her bonnet shook as she accosted me. She was dressed in black bombazine, trimmed with white lace, as usual.

"Yes," I said to her. "But how did you know?" I did not have the baby with me.

"Indeed, Hannah Chelmsford," she said, "the whole town knows he rode off without her. Are you sure you know what you're about?"

"Do any of us? Ever?"

"Don't be cocky, miss." Then she put a gloved hand on my arm, solicitously, and lowered her tone. "You have a good heart, Hannah. You always did. Everyone knows how hard you work to keep your family together. But everyone also knows how stubborn you are, how like your mother."

I drew in my breath at the mention of my mother. I was about to give a sharp retort, when she spoke again.

"I never told you this, Hannah, but personally I always admired your mother and how she held her head high and paid no mind to the busybodies when they stopped talking to her because she fed the British during the war."

But you were one of those busybodies, I thought.

"Now you may think me a meddlesome old lady, but I have some advice for you. Would you take it?"

How else would I be rid of her, unless I listened?

"You might pay a visit to your father's manufactory." The hand gripped tighter on my arm and the feathers shook again on the bonnet.

"The manufactory?" I asked. "What has it to do with the baby?"

"Nothing. And everything," she sighed. "Hannah, that man treats those manufactory girls disgracefully. Does your father know of it? A committee of us concerned women in Salem are about to close the place down if Mr. Leonard doesn't mend his ways."

"Close the manufactory down?" My head whirled. Why had I heard nothing of this? Because I'd been too busy with my own problems, which had been many.

"Yes, the home weavers are faring well, but

the girls aren't. We have paid Mr. Leonard a visit," Mrs. White went on. "We have given him warning. We *will* close him down if Mr. Leonard doesn't make amends. Take my advice, Hannah. A visit from you might convince the man to treat those girls better. It might also put you in a favorable light with the women on the committee."

I just stared at her, trying to take her meaning.

"We don't *want* to close him down, Hannah. We have discussed it at length. And we have pondered on why you haven't taken an interest in the manufactory and those poor girls."

Close the manufactory down? That would kill my father. Not to mention that it certainly wouldn't put me in his good graces when he returned. And, since I hadn't told him about Night Song yet, I certainly needed to garner all the good graces I could from him.

I watched Mrs. White walk away. It seemed that the feathers on her bonnet were still shaking. And I remembered my feelings about the woman, that in Salem she shared the privilege with God of being always right as rain about everything.

Almost as if he'd gotten wind of the conversation between me and Mrs. White, Mr. Leonard sent a note around the third week in September.

"Since I am not welcome at your house, it would certainly gratify me, and, I suspect, benefit us both, if you would pay me the honor of visiting my office at the mill in Beverly this coming Friday, at the hour of three, for tea. Your servant, Geoffrey Leonard."

There was a postscript, added with a flourish. "I would not, for your own welfare, ignore this invitation."

The cheek of the man! Not ignore the invitation! The careless scrawl on the rich vellum leaped out at me and I felt fear-quickened. Geoffrey Leonard was up to something. No doubt he knew he was in trouble with the women of Salem and was concerned. Yet he was a person who always turned every dolorous situation into an advantageous one, somehow.

If I went to see him, I must be on my guard. I did not reply immediately. I received the note on Monday and waited.

On Wednesday a letter came to me from Abby and Nate. They were back in America.

They had set sail from the Canary Islands in early August, after two months of recuperating. They had taken passage home on the brig *Lively*, and arrived in Charleston the first week in September.

"We are at Nate's father's plantation where I am learning to run the house and take charge of the servants," Abby wrote. "Yet I have plenty of time to work on my quilt and have acquired some interesting fabric from people we met on our travels.

"Nate is having another ship built this winter. Mayhap in spring you can come and visit us and bring Cabot. Or I will come north when Nate again drops anchor in Salem. But, will Father allow me to come home? Do you think he has forgiven me? Has he made mention of me in any of his letters? You must write. I yearn to hear from you. Your loving sister, Abby."

Mary Lander always said that every person had some good in them. If Mr. Leonard had any redeeming quality at all, it was that he got straight to the heart of the matter and didn't shilly-shally.

"I know you don't like me, Miss Chelmsford," he began.

"How could I? After you sent your men to try to ruin our party. Not to mention your many other indiscretions."

"I sent them to get your attention. To help you realize how the people of Salem feel about your harboring the child. Now, we both need each other, so shall we get on with it?"

"I know you need my help, Mr. Leonard. I've been told that the women of Salem are near to closing you down."

Across the rich Persian carpet in his office, he smiled at me. He stood in front of the hearth, which boasted a warm fire on this chilly September afternoon. Tea had been brought in on a silver service, by a servant. I sipped it politely. Rain slashed against the windows.

"You need my help, too." And he smiled.

"I?" And I laughed. "What could I possibly need from you? No, Mr. Leonard, I'm afraid I have the upper hand this time. You see, on the way in, I spoke to one of the mill girls. She was in a delicate condition. With child. She was pale and thin. I noted about her a careworn and submissive air. Why, she was almost frightened when I asked her about her working hours and conditions."

His back was to the fire. He flapped his coattails nervously. "I treat my workers well, Miss Chelmsford. I don't coddle them, but they are well treated."

"Indeed? Well, what this girl told me bears out the concerns of Mrs. White and her committee."

"And what did she tell you?"

"That the girls work six days a week, from before sunup until long after sunset. Twelve or fourteen hours a day at their cotton carding and spinning machines. Of course, no one outside the mill is supposed to know this. But I have long known Mrs. Haffield White to have the perceptive powers of the Almighty."

He smiled again and went to his desk and sat down to sip his tea. I could see he was trying to stay calm.

"They are strong girls, farm girls, all of them, accustomed to long hours and working in the fields. They want to work to send money home to their families. Many of them are widows from the war, with children to keep."

"Exactly, Mr. Leonard. War widows. Which is why they deserve special consideration."

He poured himself more tea and offered me another cup. I declined. He stirred in cream and sugar, took a scone, and buttered it carefully.

"If you recall, I asked you at the outset, to take an interest in the girls here in the mill," he said quietly. "You refused."

"Is that any reason to mistreat them?"

"No, but I was asking for help. I would have taken your advice in the beginning as to the treatment of the girls. There was no one else in the area to ask. No one in Salem or Beverly wanted this mill here to begin with. So you are somewhat to blame, for your indifference."

"How like you not to take the blame yourself." I sighed. "Well the people want the mill here even less now, no matter who is to blame. If Mrs. White has her way, they will close you down."

"They will close your father down, too," he reminded me.

The fire flickered on the hearth as a gust of wind rattled the windows. He looked at me steadily. And he knew I understood the enormity of that. I said nothing. I waited, for I sensed that he would now put forth his dirty scheme. Whatever it was, I did not know, but it was a scheme. I was sure of that. And it would be dirty.

"Do you take my meaning?" he asked.

"Go on," I said.

"I have every reason to suspect that you want

your father to be happy with you when he returns. Am I correct, Miss Chelmsford?"

"I always wish to make my father happy," I said.

"Shall I lay my cards on the table?"

"Please do."

"Very well. The busybodies of Salem have let it be known to me that the only thing that will keep them from closing the mill down is if you make regular visits here and take an interest in the girls."

I was shocked. "Mrs. White did not say that to me."

He smiled. "As a self-appointed guardian of the community's morals, she expects certain things from you, as she expects certain things from me. I, however, knew you would not volunteer to take an interest in this place unless I had the right card up my sleeve. I believe I have it."

"Do you now?"

"Yes. The baby."

I felt my heart begin to race. "What has she to do with this?"

"Have you told your father about her yet?"

"That's my business!"

"What makes you think he will allow you to keep her, when he returns? An Indian baby?"

"She is half-white."

"I am afraid that he will see her as half-Indian."

I scowled. "How can you be so sure? How can you be so certain he won't accept her, no matter what she is?"

He leaned forward and glowered at me. "Like he accepted your brother Cabot?"

I felt myself flush and go weak with anger. So he did know about that! I was a fool to think he wouldn't. The man was the kind who made sure he knew all the weak points about his enemies. And I knew, by then, that I was at least an adversary if not an enemy.

"Things have heated up on the frontier," he said. "Has your father not written to you?"

"Say your piece, Mr. Leonard. Play your last card."

To my surprise, he got up again and went to stand in front of the hearth, this time with his back to me. He stared into the fire for a moment. "I wish I did not have to be the one to tell you this." And his voice was tight now, and sad. Then he turned to face me and I saw that he was genuinely distressed.

"I received a letter late last week from your father, Miss Hannah," he said sadly. "And I truly wish I did not have to tell you this."

He went back to his desk, pulled open a drawer and took out the letter. "Your father writes in this missive that your sister Thankful has been taken, Miss Hannah. This is why I called you here today. I know how fond you are of that baby. This is why I said we can now help each other."

I stared up at him. He had come to stand over me. He was holding out the letter. Taken? What did he mean, taken?

"If you agree to take an interest in the girls here, if you save the mill, I will write to your father. I will convince him that taking in the baby, giving it a home, will make known to all the public-spirited intentions of the man who is part owner of Beverly Cotton Manufactory."

I did not understand his words. They came from very far away and all I could hear was a buzzing in my ears.

"Taken?" I asked. "What do you mean Thankful was taken? By whom?"

"Why, by Indians, Miss Hannah. The child is gone. No one knows where she is. That is the whole point in my summoning you here this day. We can *help* each other. You need me now. How will your father ever permit you to keep a half-Indian baby when his own daughter was kidnapped by Indians?"

The buzzing in my ears grew louder. Then every-thing went dark and I felt myself slipping into the darkness, grateful for its embrace, grateful that I did not have to listen to this man's terrible words any longer.

The last words I heard were the ones he yelled to his servant. Something about bringing brandy. The last thought I had was that this was the second time since I'd known him that Mr. Leonard's words were sending me into oblivion.

Chapter Eighteen

Cold September rain slashed with a vengeance against the windows of my room. In the half-light of morning I was aware of Mattie creeping in, setting down my morning chocolate and biscuit, and saying my name. I murmured a response into the pillow.

"There's a letter here for you," she said. "It came late in yesterday's post. You ran right to bed yesterday when John Gardener drove you home from Beverly. You looked as if the Devil himself was chasing you. Are you sick, Hannah?"

"A letter?" I sat up. My mind came awake. Something was wrong. What?

And then it was as if a wet blanket were thrown over me. And I was cold and suffocating.

Thankful was gone. Taken by Indians.

I looked up at Mattie's face, innocent of knowledge of this matter yet. As was all of my household. I glanced down at the letter on the tray.

"It's from your father," she said. Her tone had

the reverence in it she usually reserved for my father, though she did not like him.

So he was writing to tell me of Thankful's disappearance then. Finally, *after* he'd written to Leonard! I nodded and said nothing. I felt a bile rising in my throat. How like Father to write to his business partner before me!

"What's wrong, Hannah?" Mattie asked. "Something *is* wrong, I know it! Margaret's hurt sore that you locked yourself in your room yesterday and wouldn't touch the tray I brought up. Have you taken a chill? Are you feverish?"

I shook my head, no. From downstairs came the morning smells of frying bacon and coffee. I heard Margaret calling after Cabot to put on his oilskins and hurry or he'd be late for school.

"I took a chill in the storm and was feeling poorly," I lied.

"It's a bad one, all right. Looks as if it's working itself up to be a nor'easter."

"Yes. I'm all right now, Mattie. Just stoke the fire up and leave me be with my chocolate and Father's letter."

She did not believe me for a moment, but she did my bidding.

"How is the baby?" I asked.

She set the poker down. "She's keeping, Hannah. Why shouldn't she be?"

I nodded. "I want to bathe her this morning. Tell Margaret to build up the fire in the kitchen and heat the water. I'll bathe her right after breakfast."

She eyed me carefully with Richard's knowing gaze. I can't fool her, I minded, she knows something's amiss. You can't fool any of the Landers. God, how I missed Richard. I felt the missing of him like a sickness inside me. My soul expanded, reaching out to him, wanting him here. And then recoiled inward on itself, like a flower, dying. And I felt like a part of me was missing. Richard would know what to do. He would help me now, as he'd helped me with Cabot.

But he wasn't here. And so I must make my way through this nightmare alone. I sighed, and looked again at Mattie. She was waiting. I saw her bottom lip thrust out, in that way that Richard had of doing when he wanted to be stubborn. I can't tell her yet, I minded. I won't tell anyone until I read the letter. I must see the awful truth in my father's writing before I go telling anyone.

"Leave me," I said. "I want to read my father's letter. I'll be down shortly."

She left. I picked up my cup of hot chocolate and tried to keep myself from shivering. It *would* be storming on a morning like this. But inside me the storm was worse. My memories of yesterday's events assaulted me with all the fury of the wind and rain raging outside.

I gave myself a moment to sip the chocolate. It was steaming hot and it soothed me. In a moment

I stopped trembling and was able to pick up the letter.

My Dear Hannah: It grieves me to have to send such news. But your sister Thankful is missing. She seems to have dropped off the ends of the earth. Dear God, I cannot bring myself to even write these words to you! But I must.

I felt myself go weak as the familiar scrawl leaped off the pages at me. I had to stop reading and lean back on my pillows and stare for a moment at the torrents of rain streaming down the windows. Then I went on reading.

We left for Louisantville the third week in July. The decision was to leave Thankful at Maysville, but she made such a fuss, wanting to come along. Lawrence said we should take her with us, and we shouldn't make others responsible for her. Indeed, she threatened to run off if we left her with friends, and follow. And you know how headstrong she is.

All was fine the first week of our journey and the weather was with us. As you know I was to start a store in Louisantville. Our camps at night were secure and we were within five miles of Louisantville one especially sunny morning. Our guides assured us that the region was safe.

Thankful was riding her own horse and dropped back to pick some flowers. We must have traveled about five miles with her riding a little behind us. Every so often I heard her voice as she talked to her horse. She was so happy. Never have I seen a child take to the wilderness so. She seems to have been born to it.

Oh, Hannah, I can scarcely write these words! After a while I realized I did not hear her voice anymore and called ahead to Lawrence and the others. Lawrence doubled back to look for his sister. "I thought you were watching her," he said to me. He was quite angry with me, Hannah, and deservedly so. For I am afraid my mind was wandering, thinking about my business ventures, and not thinking of her.

As it happened, Lawrence could not find her. None of us could, though we immediately organized a search party and spread out and called her name and fired our muskets. The lovely scenery mocked us, as the hills echoed our calls and only silence followed. We searched the region for a circumference of five miles. We camped out on the spot that night and kept fires lit all night long. It was as if the earth opened to swallow her.

Then Lawrence, who has become quite adept at these things, found Indian footprints in an area where her bouquet of wildflowers was strewn all about. . . .

The letter went on, with questions, ruminations, self-recriminations, and prophesies that he would go mad if Thankful were not soon found. I set the pages aside. My head throbbed by now. I could not believe it was true.

My sister. Gone. My sister taken by Indians. My mind would not take that next step which meant conjecturing about how they would treat her, what they would do to her.

My mind, for the moment, was paralyzed. What would I do? I closed my eyes. Richard, I whispered, help me.

I waited. In the darkness behind my lids I conjured up Richard. I saw him standing there in front of me. *Richard!* I saw the sea then, endless and white-capped, but calm, and the outline of the *Black Prince* on the stretch of waters.

I heard the sound of my own breathing, becoming more and more calm. And then I heard the voice inside me, Richard's voice.

Don't allow yourself to think such, Hannah. You must believe that Thankful will survive. She's a brazen little piece, remember? She has courage. Don't despair, or you'll go mad. Trust that Thankful will be found. Or you will fall into that black hole. And then there will be no one to take care of your family.

I opened my eyes and looked around my room, half expecting to see the ghost of him there. For a moment he had seemed so close to me! But all I saw were my familiar things, the walls I'd papered with the printed liners of China tea chests, the deep window seats, the crisp white curtains, my books, the likeness of Mama that Lawrence had painted. I took strength from them.

And I made my decision then and there. I must trust that Thankful would be found. Or I would go mad. And then there would be no one to take care of the family. I would go about my daily life, taking one day at a time. And trusting in the next one.

And so I got out of bed and put on my morning wrapper and went downstairs.

I will have breakfast, I told myself, as I descended the stairway. Then I will tell Mattie and Margaret that Thankful is missing. Then I will bathe and dress Night Song. I will take my strength from her, from the way she smiles at me, from the way I see all of the stars in her eyes, all the hope of humankind there, as such hope is mirrored in every baby's eyes, if only we choose to see it. I will take strength from the way she reaches out to me and gurgles and laughs.

And then I will dress warmly and have John Gardener drive me back to Beverly. I will take a basket of food for the girls at the mill. I will talk with them at their noon meal and try to come up with a plan to help them. I may even, in the days ahead, visit the women weaving cotton in their homes.

I will save my father's mill for him. And by

doing so, I will make a place here for Night Song. When my father hears how I saved the mill, he will allow me to keep the child.

Mr. Leonard will write to him and convince him to let me keep her. Yes, I will go along with this plan. It will work for the benefit of us all.

It did not come to me then that I was agreeing to keep the mill from closing so I could keep the baby. And that the last time I made such a trade I gave up Thankful, allowing her to be taken west, so Abby could run away with Nate.

Nor did it come to me that I might be trying to keep the mill alive for my father, because I was blaming myself for allowing Thankful to go west. And I had to make matters up to him.

All these thoughts would haunt me later. At the moment all I knew was what I had always known, that I would do anything to save my family. And that there was no longer any doubt in my mind that baby Night Song was a part of it.

Chapter Nineteen

A week later, on a bright and breezy afternoon, I asked John Gardener to drive me to Beverly, for a visit with Mr. Leonard. As the carriage took me over the newly opened Essex Bridge, I planned what I would say. I would be strong. I would offer help at the mill, but I must remember not to put myself in the position of a supplicant.

By that same token, however, I must allow him his pride. This must work out as an agreement from which we both benefited.

A difficult task, because I was angry over what I'd learned in the past week. I alighted from the carriage in front of the three-story brick building on an open tract of land in North Beverly. I looked up at the sign that swung over the office door. *Beverly Cotton Manufactory*, it said. The letters were printed in gold.

What I had learned from two previous visits here in the last week was what I had suspected all along. That Mr. Geoffrey Leonard was an imperious man who bullied his workers, and who never did a thing that was not calculated to put money into his own pocket.

The girls who worked in this place were ill-clad, ill-fed, careworn, and impoverished of spirit. It had taken all my efforts to get them to trust me enough to speak of their lives, which were bereft of all but the bare necessities. The home weavers were not adequately paid.

In short, the mill was everything Lawrence and I feared it would be. But the fault was very much mine. I minded that, standing and looking up at that sign. I had ignored the mill, sidestepped my responsibility.

But what was I about now, lending myself and my blessings to this place? How could I ever hope to induce Leonard to change his ways? I had a moment's panic, in which I drew back. But it was only for a moment. Then I came to my senses and went inside.

"I have decided to assist you in the management of the girls in the mill, Mr. Leonard."

"How kind of you, Miss Chelmsford."

"Yes. I have been thinking on the matter. I would like to do something about getting them some new clothing. There are several merchants in town who might be convinced to donate some fabric. Of course, the girls could sew the clothing themselves. I could show them how."

"Splendid!"

"It would not do for young women working in

an establishment in which my father has a partnership to look as they do. Why their mode of dress beggars all description! They do not have clothing of sufficient warmth for winter."

"You are most kind."

"I understand you are boarding the girls at Miss Thrumbell's establishment here in North Beverly."

"Yes, she is very neat and clean."

"But she does not know how to cook for so many. And you have not provided her with the means to do so, though you take money out of the girls' pay for room and board."

"The meals are adequate, Miss Chelmsford. I have, on occasion, dined there myself."

"So have I, this past week, Mr. Leonard. The meal was anything but adequate. I would ask you to increase the woman's allowance for food."

"Increase the allowance?"

"Yes. I shall pay her another visit. With Margaret, our housekeeper and cook. Margaret could share her knowledge about making nourishing soups and stews. Margaret is a Scotswoman. You know how frugal they are."

"I do, indeed!"

"And if you increase the food allowance, I am sure I could get Reverend Bentley, the faithful and devoted pastor of East Church, who ministers to all of Salem, to put Miss Thrumbell's establishment on his list to receive an occasional food basket."

"That would be most kind of you, Miss Chelmsford."

"Now, as for leisure time, Mr. Leonard. We must discuss it."

"Leisure time?"

"Yes. The girls should have a longer time for their noon meal. And perhaps start an hour later in the cold winter months. Or leave an hour sooner."

"But my dear Miss Chelmsford, that is most irregular in an establishment such as this. It is my experience that the lower classes do not know how to use leisure time."

"Many of them have children. I think they would know what to do with an hour more a day, Mr. Leonard. Now, about church."

"Church?"

"Yes. I understand you force the mill girls to attend and support St. Peter's Episcopal, your own church. I understand you take church donations out of their pay, though some of the girls are Congregationalist."

"You understand wrong, Miss Chelmsford! I would never force my religion on anyone!"

"Good. Then you will allow them to go to their own churches?"

"Of course!"

"And, in that same spirit, you would allow Reverend Bentley to come and visit the girls here sometimes?"

"For what purpose, Miss Chelmsford?"

"For the purpose of being a friend to them. A friend who might speak to them of the dignity of human nature. A friend who might, betimes, read to them as they take their noon meal. A friend who might acquaint them with the blessings of our newfound liberty."

"Liberty?"

"Yes, Mr. Leonard. You may recollect, it is what we fought for in the recent unpleasantness between your people and mine. It is what some of the husbands of your workers died for. Do you not think they should become acquainted with its blessings?"

"By all means, yes."

"Perhaps Reverend Bentley may offer to take the children of your workers on his nature walks. I trust you have no objections to this?"

"None, Miss Chelmsford."

"Good. This is a beginning, Mr. Leonard. Now, if you will agree to raise the stipend you pay the home weavers, I shall now be able to report to Mrs. Haffield White and her committee the progress we have made here today. And assure them that at sometime in the near future, they may pay you another visit and bestow upon you their blessings for your benevolence and your lofty integrity."

He looked shaken, but he agreed. "Such a visit would be most welcome, Miss Chelmsford. Meanwhile, I am happy to report to you that I wrote to your father in this last week. I told him about the child. And how it would be in the best interests of the Beverly Cotton Manufactory if it were to get about town that he, the financial backer and part owner of this mill, was a patron of this motherless babe."

"Thank you, Mr. Chelmsford."

"Some trappers I know were making the trip west. The letter should get to him soon."

"This visit has been most beneficial to us both, Mr. Leonard. I am glad I came."

I went once a week to the mill that fall. I taught the girls to sew their new clothing with fabric I had personally requisitioned from local merchants. I visited Miss Thrumbell's boarding establishment, with Margaret in tow. We sat with that good woman over tea and discussed recipes.

Sometimes we brought a basket from the grocer with Reverend Bentley's best respects. In it were bakers' flour loaves or pans of gingerbread. Another time it might be butter, cheese, and eggs. Or tea and sugar and a big salt fish and fresh apples.

Margaret taught Miss Thrumbell how to make a good, nourishing fish stew, corn cakes, to roast a side of pork over the open hearth, and make a good roast mutton. We discovered that the beds, though furnished with clean linen, needed quilts. It would be a cold winter in Massachusetts. Boston Harbor had frozen over three times last winter.

I had only to tell Mrs. White of the quilt problem and in a week had a dozen good quilts to donate to Miss Thrumbell's.

Reverend Bentley sent around a wagonload of wood for the boardinghouse hearths.

And so I spent the waning days of that year, running errands, visiting the home weavers and mill, teaching the girls to sew, working with Reverend Bentley and Mrs. White to make life bearable for the girls who worked in my father's mill.

By Christmas I was near exhaustion. A few days after Christmas I was enjoying a night in front of my own hearth, a rare pleasure. Night Song had been put to bed. Cabot was doing his schoolwork on the rug, when there came a knocking on the door on this drizzly, cold night.

I was expecting no one.

Cabot looked at me, then went to answer the door. In a moment he was back in the parlor, looking like he'd seen a ghost.

I looked at him. "Who is it?"

"It's Father," he croaked. "He's home."

Living in Salem, a port town in which there were wrenching departures and unexpected homecomings every day, I suppose I should have been accustomed to surprising knocks on the door by now. But I wasn't. I probably never would be. And I felt myself go limp at Cabot's announcement. For of all the homecomings I could expect, I looked forward to this one the least of all.

Chapter Twenty

He appeared so much older. His shoulders were bent. There was a frailness about him that had not been there before. His voice was a bit weaker, his hair all gray. He had a persistent cough. And there seemed to be a peculiar fire burning inside him. At first I thought it to be fever.

I became fear-quickened, thinking he was gravely ill. We put him right to bed that first evening. He barely spoke except to say that he had come alone. He had left his guides in Pennsylvania and rode home alone by horse in the rain and the cold. He had spent Christmas Day on the road.

And he murmured one more thing to us as we piled the quilts around him.

"Lawrence sent me home," he said. "He made me come. I didn't want to."

That alone should have told me that my father had changed. Before he left on this trip he wouldn't have listened to Lawrence if my brother had suddenly developed the gift of second sight.

Now Lawrence had ordered him home. And he had obeyed.

I was afraid, as I looked at his pale face on the pillow, that he was a broken and defeated man.

I was wrong. It would take more than what he had been through to break my father. The first two days, indeed, he was ailing. He stayed in bed. Margaret made him special soups. Everyone walked on tiptoe. Neighbors and friends called and left cards.

By the third day he was on his feet, having breakfast with us, planning on going back to his counting house that morning. And visiting his favorite coffee house. And the mill. Though he was still spent and feverish.

He would not listen to our admonitions. He ordered the carriage and John Gardener came to drive him where he wanted to go.

Three things I noticed about him that first morning he was on his feet again. He spoke naught of his trip. He did not mention Thankful. And though we made no attempt to keep Night Song out of his sight, he acted as if the child were a piece of furniture. He would not acknowledge her.

I stood watching him climb into the carriage as he left for his counting house. It was snowing lightly. It is as if he has left a part of him out west, I minded. Will he ever speak of Thankful? Does he blame me?

Mid-afternoon, the end of the business day for

Salem's merchants, he returned home. He went into the parlor, ordered a glass of Madeira, and called for me.

I stood in front of him. "Yes, Father?"

He looked at me, up and down, as if he'd never seen me before. "Tonight, after supper, we will talk," he said.

It was a summons, nothing less. I was to give an accounting of myself. I nodded, yes. And I felt a numbness in my bones.

I tried that evening to act with decorum all through supper. I let Father do all the talking. It was at supper that he first mentioned Lawrence.

"I agreed to come home only if he stayed to look for your sister. After all, it was his suggestion we not leave her in Maysville. So he will stay until she is found."

I saw the dismay on Cabot's face. But Mattie received that news with more difficulty. Standing over Father's shoulder with a tureen of soup, she had all she could do to keep from dropping it. Her face went white and she set the tureen down and ran from the room.

Father frowned. "That girl will simply have to accept that Lawrence won't be back for a while. Never did understand why Lawrence fancies her. But he gets downright stubborn when I say such to him." He shrugged. "Between you and your brother, our fortunes are irrevocably tied in with the Landers, aren't they?"

"Our fortunes were tied in with the Landers family long before Lawrence and I had anything to do with it," I said.

Our eyes met. Our gazes locked. So, you intend to be feisty, my girl, do you? he was thinking. Well, I hope you can take as well as you give. I knew him. And I was determined to be equal to him, whatever he said.

When we finished our dessert and he announced that we should go into the parlor, I stood up to face him. "First, I must see the baby to bed," I said. "I will be down shortly."

He nodded and I went to put Night Song in her cradle. The rhythms of the household did not break because of Father's homecoming. And they revolved around Night Song, as in every household in which there is a baby.

When I came down I found Father reading his newspaper before a cheery fire in the parlor. Cabot had taken up a book. They were not talking.

I brought forth a square of fabric from my quilt. As luck would have it, I had been working on stitching Mother's name in the middle of the blue wool from the British naval officer's coat. I saw no reason to put it aside. If Father took note of it he chose to ignore it.

"You've heard of the attacks on the frontier," he said as I sat down.

"Yes."

"I have nothing but praise for the Kentuckians

who are renewing their expeditions to wipe out the Shawnees. I intend to write a long memoir to Secretary of War, Henry Knox, outlining a way to overwhelm them by military force."

I thought of Night Song's mother, killed by Kentuckians, but said nothing.

"I've given up my idea of a trading post on the frontier," Father went on. "I'm going to keep my hand in shipping. But only to work the coastwise commerce with smaller schooners and sloops. I'll leave the transoceanic trade routes to the Derbys and Crowninshields. And to Richard Lander."

I still kept my silence.

"And I intend to build up my mill. Geoffrey heard tell of a young man named Slater who posted a letter from London to a New York cotton manufactory before he boarded a ship for this country. This Slater is carrying, in his very excellent memory, the plans for a cotton mill, right out of England."

"I still don't like mills, Father. But we have an agreement, your Geoffrey and I."

He glowered at me. "Do you not hear what I am saying, Hannah? Britain forbids the export of textile machinery or any designs for it. And Slater has it all memorized in his head! He is looking for a job as a mill manager. I intend to meet with the man and make use of his talents. I hear that Moses Brown of Rhode Island also has the same idea. I can only hope Brown doesn't get to him first."

I sighed. "Is that what you wished to discuss with me?"

"No," he glowered. Then he looked at Cabot. "Has your game of chess improved at all, boy?"

"I've no one to practice with since Captain Nate left."

"That damned Southerner couldn't play if his life depended on it. Go get the board, boy."

"Father! For shame!" I chided. "It was Nate's superb seamanship that saved them in the wreck. I should think you'd be grateful for that."

"Damned slaveholder. Better never come back to Salem."

"I'm sure he will, Father, and that he'll bring Abby."

"He can bring half of South Carolina with him for all I care. Neither of them is welcome in this house. I'll have nothing to do with a daughter who defied her father and went off to marry a slaveholder. She chose him over me. Now let her live with her choice."

I kept my good counsel for a minute. Cabot returned and began setting up the board. Thank heavens he missed *that* exchange, I told myself.

"Your mood is more vile than usual this evening," I said. "Is this why you asked us to sit with you? To spew out your anger on us?"

"No. Because there are too many stagnant waters in this house. And we're drifting in them. We need a strong westerly, to get us moving again.

Need to go over the ships' logs and note the quirks in the currents. Go ahead, boy, make your move, don't dream over it."

Cabot moved his man on the board. And for a while they played out their game of chess, in some silent minuet, before the light of the fire. I said nothing while the game was in progress. Father loved his chess and he did not like to talk during the game. When finally he made his last move on the board, he sat back triumphantly.

"Whoever taught you chess, you've still a thing or two to learn, hey?" he asked.

Cabot got up. "You taught me," he reminded him.

Father grunted. "Time for bed. Your sister and I have serious talking to do."

Cabot kissed me goodnight. I saw the concern in his eyes and gave him a reassuring smile.

"He's growing up," Father said as Cabot left the room.

"Yes."

"I'd like to know about that money that's been put in my ledgers in his name, Hannah."

I paused for a minute, thinking. Two matters were in the front of my mind. It went without saying that I had to give an accounting of myself to him, but I had run the household for near a year without his advice, and I chafed under the obligation of once again assuming the role of dutiful daughter.

But more than that, we had not spoken of Night

Song yet. And I knew in my bones that her future in this house depended upon the outcome of this talk between us.

"The money is for Cabot's education," I answered.

"His education, is it? And how did the money get into my ledgers?"

"It's from a benefactor. Richard took care of the matter before he left."

"Well? Am I not to know who this benefactor is?"

"I think you know, Father."

"Look at me, girl. Yes, I know. It's Burnaby, isn't it? Well, tell me!"

I looked up. He'd come to stand over me. He towered over me. Tall, so tall, and the one blue eye and the one green one bore into my very soul. I was frightened by what I saw in those eyes. But I must stand up for Cabot, I reminded myself. And in doing so, I knew I would be standing up for Night Song, this very minute sleeping on her stomach in her cradle upstairs, her little fists clenched against the terrors of the world.

"Yes, it's Burnaby," I said. So he'd known the name of the man mother had given herself to then. He'd known it all along.

Chapter Twenty-one

"You think you are clever, running circles around me," he asked, "don't you?"

"I don't think I'm clever at all, Father."

"You maneuvered your sister's elopement under my nose. Well, she's gone now, so don't cry to me about it. You convinced me to take Thankful west. And now she's gone."

I drew in my breath. So he *was* going to blame me for Thankful. "Am I to take all of the blame for what's happened to this family?" I asked.

"You meddle, Hannah."

"Meddle? I try to help! You left me in charge, always, to do your bidding to run the house while you took the credit for the good things that happened. But when your children had problems, they came to me. I helped them as best I could, Father. I'm sorry if I failed. But at least I tried. At least they had someone to come to in me."

"Are you saying they didn't have their father?"

For a moment I thought he would strike me, as he had my mother. His face went red, then white.

He was capable of doing it. I saw his jaw twitch. Then, of a sudden, he turned and went to stand and look out the window into the freezing blackness.

"There are too many ghosts in this damned room," he said.

I allowed him his moment of misery.

"It's no simple chore to be a father." He turned to look at me. "Do you think I did not attempt to discharge my duties properly?"

"I never said such."

"Mistakes are made. A man should be able to live them down and not be haunted by them."

"Perhaps first a man should acknowledge them," I said.

"And if I did? Would you acknowledge that you deserve some of the blame then, too, Hannah?"

"I have been tormenting myself for blame all along, Father, if it makes you happy to know such," I snapped.

He nodded. Then he sighed. "But to go and accept money from that blasted king's man for Cabot's education! It galls me, to have his money in my accounts."

"He offered it. I saw no reason to decline. It's for Cabot, not for you. The man is at least honoring his responsibilities."

"Are you saying that I haven't, with the boy?"

"Only you can answer that, Father."

He scowled, looked about to give an angry retort, then changed his mind. "I suppose Burnaby has told him he's his father, then." His face was ashen, his voice frail, suddenly.

I stared up at him. "No," I said.

"You told him, then? Or Richard? Cabot knows the truth. I can see it in his eyes when he looks at me."

"He knows only that you are not his father. But not because anyone here informed him of that fact." I told him about Thankful's letter.

He absorbed the telling with no expression. "I never should have confided in Thankful. How did he take it, being so informed?"

"How do you think?"

"I never wanted him to know. I know you won't believe that."

"I believe it, though I think it would have been kinder if you'd told him instead of treating him so shabbily. And I think you should be the one to tell him now, who his father is."

He nodded gravely. "I curse that British cur who ruined my marriage."

"Burnaby didn't ruin your marriage, Father. You did."

"What? You can say that to me, after he admitted to you what happened between him and your mother?"

My face burned with the need of what I must do. "You ruined your own marriage," I said, "Burnaby told me everything, including how you sometimes struck her."

He looked about to explode. Then, seeing I

would not back down, his arrogance collapsed, like a sail suddenly bereft of wind. "I loved her," he said. "I was beset, at times with demons. It didn't mean I didn't love her."

I sighed. "Do you think that makes what you did to her, right?" I asked.

"Do you think that justifies her unfaithfulness?"

I was trembling. "You could have honored her memory for her children after she was gone."

"That's too much to ask of a wronged man, Hannah."

"As it was too much to ask that you accept Cabot?"

An insidious smile appeared on his face. "Do you think your Richard is going to accept another man's baby?" he asked. "Have you considered *that* at all?"

Chapter Twenty-two

It was the first mention he had made of Night Song. So, I thought, we are now at the crux of the matter.

"I don't object to your marrying Richard," he said. "He has shown true Yankee ingenuity in the way he restored the *Prince*. And there is talk about town that he will prove to be a successful Salem shipowner and merchant."

"That is decent of you, Father."

He did not belabor my sarcasm. "He has worked long and hard to vanquish the ghosts in his past. I admire a man who can do that. But will you now make him inherit more ghosts, Hannah? Do you think I don't know what you are about, with this baby? You are trying to make right in this house what never was right before. She is Cabot, all over again, this child, isn't she?"

I ran my tongue along my lips, which had gone dry. "No," I said. "She isn't. That isn't why I want to raise her."

"Why then, Hannah?"

"I'm doing it for Louis. And for the child who has no home."

"You're doing it for your mother," he said. He thrust his hands into his trouser pockets and began to pace up and down in front of the hearth, nervously.

I found my voice. "Perhaps you are right, Father," I agreed.

"It's what you've been trying to do all along," he elaborated, "make up for matters that never can be right in this family. Things happen to people in life, Hannah. Terrible things, that change people, that sometimes ruin families. You can't set yourself up above such things and try to make them as before. It doesn't work."

"What's the harm in trying? Especially if some good comes out of it?"

"The harm, Hannah, is that you hurt everyone trying. You open old wounds. You go against the tide. You prevent the healing. And who's to say good will come out of you taking in this child? What will you do if Richard doesn't accept her?"

"He will," I said.

"Will he? I tried, Hannah. I could never accept another man's child. I could never accept Cabot." His face was screwed up and bitter as he said it. "And what if she never accepts herself? What if she can't be made into a proper Salem woman? She's part savage. Have you thought of that?"

I continued sewing.

He eyed my handiwork sadly. "Where is the fabric from Leonard?"

"I will not include it in my quilt, Father, don't ask it of me."

"You never give up, do you, Hannah? But you've kept the fabric from Burnaby's coat. And you're stitching it into that quilt of yours, as if you can stitch up all the ragged pieces of the past and make it whole again."

"I must try, Father," I said. "Please. You must let me try. You must let me keep the child. Perhaps I won't have to raise her. Louis might be home in a year or so. Then he can take her back to her people."

"Don't count on that," he said.

Something in the way he said it made me take note. "Why?"

"Because her own people won't want her—half white as she is. And because I've asked Louis to search for your sister, too. He knows his way around out there, with both the whites and the Indians. He's on good terms with Blue Jacket and many other Indian chiefs."

I felt the wind go out of me. "Because he married one of their own," I said in wonderment. "And you are taking advantage of that."

"Yes. I will take advantage of anything to get your sister back. Louis is my one good hope, as a matter of fact."

"And how long has he agreed to search for her, Father?"

"For as long as it takes."

"I see." I bent my head over my sewing again, taking strength from the mere fact of having something to do.

"And he is doing this for you, then, and you object to his child in your house?" I asked.

He was watching me stitch Mother's name, his eyes fixed on the lettering. "No," he said quietly. "We made an agreement, he and I, much the same as you made with Leonard. Leonard told me of it."

My heart quickened. "What agreement did you make with Louis?"

"When I met Louis out there and he told me you took the child, I was not happy about it. But I told him I would keep her in my house, allow you to raise her, as long as he looked for my daughter."

My eyes widened. "You made him agree to this? You held his daughter's security over his head?"

"In return for *my* daughter's security, Hannah."

I could not believe it! "Then all the while, you were willing to take in Night Song! And I made the agreement with Mr. Leonard for nothing!"

He smiled wryly. "Are you sorry for the agreement? Leonard got you to take an interest in the mill, I hear, something you should have done a long time ago."

My face flamed. "Do you know *why*, Father? Because Mrs. White and friends were going to close it down, if I didn't step in on behalf of the women Leonard was treating so shabbily. Did he tell you *that*?"

He stared at me. *"Mrs. White?"*

"Yes. Your Geoffrey said he would apprise you of the benefits of taking in the child if I would help the women he'd so mistreated that he was about to be closed down."

He scowled. "Why didn't someone tell me of this?"

"I'm sure Mrs. White will, sooner or later, Father."

He was silent for a moment. And I took a malicious delight in the anguish I knew this news was causing him.

"I never intended for the mill workers to be mistreated, Hannah," he said sadly. "I thank you for what you did. You may keep the child, of course. But I'll have naught to do with her. I have had too many blows to the heart."

"What kind of household will it be then, until I can marry Richard and take her away?"

"You raised Cabot here," he said, "didn't you?" And he touched me on the shoulder. "Margaret tells me there must be a christening. Do it in spring. I shall invite my friends."

I nodded. "I see. You intend, then, to use the child to show everyone the extent of your moral integrity and your lofty ideals."

"I intend to invite my friends," he said. "I want no expense spared for the occasion."

"Very well. We have an agreement, Father. I'm so glad we had this little talk this evening."

He smiled dourly. "You play as bad a game of chess as your brother," he said. And then he left the room.

Chapter Twenty-three

September 1789

The christening was put off until the last week in September. One thing or another interfered. In April my father went to New York for Washington's inauguration and later met with Slater. Then with the onset of summer many of the people he wanted to invite left town for their country estates, or farms. That last week in September a storm raged over the whole coast of Salem and Beverly and Marblehead for two days. The morning of the christening it turned to snow.

My father had invited half the town to the christening, it seemed. Six extra girls were hired to help Margaret and Mattie. John Gardener was given a whole new set of proper livery and the house was in a turmoil of preparation for a week.

In spite of the storm, everyone came. Food was in abundance and Father even hired local musicians. I and Cabot were little Georgianna's godparents. The back parlor was filled with gifts for the child, who was toddling around by now. And

Father basked in the congratulations from his merchant friends.

But he did not pick up Georgianna. He did not touch her. I was accustomed to this by now. What I was not accustomed to was the way he was using the child for his own selfish purposes.

"I can't abide it," I told Mary Lander.

"Your father has used people all his life, Hannah," she said. "Accept the good and be glad for it. Most times if you look into the reasons a person does good, you will be disappointed. Most people have selfish reasons."

I minded that it was more fitting for Mary Lander to say that than anyone. But I felt miserable, just the same.

It was getting on to four in the afternoon when the knock came on the door. It was already dark outside, though the house was ablaze with candles. I was passing through the center hall when John Gardener opened it.

A man stood there in oilskins. Outside the wind was blowing in gale force and he dripped water in a puddle around him in the hall.

"I have been told that Mr. Joseph Hiller, custom's officer, is in this house," he said. "I have a message for him."

"I will give it to him." I stepped forward. Something in the way the man stood there, lantern in hand, made me take notice. The look of him, the long dour face, the way he had made his way to us in the storm, all boded no good.

"Mr. Hiller should know," the man said in a manner that was a pronouncement, nothing less, "that rumor is quickly spreading through Salem this day. Richard Lander has been seen in town!"

My hand flew to my throat. I felt the floor move under me. And it seemed that all the candles flickered, suddenly. "Richard is back?"

"Aye." And the man fastened his dour gaze upon me as he accepted a cup of hot cider from one of the hired servant girls and gulped it down. "But there are those who say it is his ghost."

And he uttered the words loud enough so they echoed in the hall. The man had a sense of drama. Either that, or he sensed the importance of his message and he wanted attention.

He soon got it. Word spread like wildfire and guests started crowding into the hall to gaze at the man.

My father stepped forward. "We're celebrating here today," he said. "I thank you for your message and invite you to the kitchen for a plate of food. But we all know that in such weather as we're having, tales like this circulate. Tales of ships wrenched to pieces offshore, of vessels breaking at the seams under the pounding seas. Such tales run rife through Salem in storms."

But the messenger was not to be robbed of his moment. " 'Tis no tale," he said. "I've seen this man himself, be he Richard Lander or not."

"Richard? Is Richard back?" Mary Lander came forward. The people parted to let her through.

Mattie was with her. "Tell me," Mary begged the visitor, "did you see him? Did you see my Richard?"

The man handed the cup back to the waiting serving girl. "Thank ye kindly," he said to her. Then he looked at Mary Lander. "There are some who sit in coffee houses and ordinaries this day and claim it is Lander in the flesh, they've seen. That he's driven the *Black Prince* ashore and dropped anchor near Winter Island. And visited one tavern after another in town to try to get a message to the custom's officer."

Mary let out a cry of joy. Mattie hushed her.

"And he awaits that officer now on Winter Island!" The messenger's voice rose above the murmur of inquiry from the crowd. "Is Mr. Hiller here?"

"I'm here." And the man came into the hall.

I thought I would faint. I felt the closeness of the people around me, closing in on me.

"Where is he?" Mr. Hiller asked. "In Salem's coffee houses or on Winter Island?"

"There are those," the messenger said, "who claim that the man who came to the Sun Tavern today to order a bowl of turtle soup and rum, was no ghost and no castaway. But Richard Lander, returned after thirteen months at sea."

I let out a cry then. Mattie came and put her arm around my shoulder.

The man in oilskins looked into the faces of the crowd. "I was in the Sun Tavern." He reached inside his oilskins and drew out a gold coin. "And the man who calls himself Richard Lander gave me this." He held up a strange-looking coin.

Reverend Bentley stepped forward. "May I see that, please?"

The man handed it over.

Reverend Bentley held it up to the light. He put the coin between his teeth and bit down on it. "Gold!" he said.

Our guests gasped.

"But," Mr. Hiller, who was a short and plump man, said, holding up his hand, "I put forth that a prudent ship's master who found his ship in such waters in this time would keep well offshore and not attempt to drop anchor. Lest he be dismasted and broken to pieces."

More murmurs from the crowd.

"And I," said my father, "say that Richard Lander could not possibly be returned to us so soon. As one of his investors, I know his destination. It is impossible that he can be back."

I heard the intake of my own breath. *My father, one of Richard's investors!* Through the sea of faces in the hallway my eyes met his and he smiled at me, smugly.

No, I thought.

Yes, those eyes seemed to say. Did you think I would not back him? I know a good thing when I see it.

I felt a sense of dismay. A sense of dread. But I did not know why.

"What was his destination?" someone asked. "Tell us!"

"Yes, tell us," someone else said. And a murmur of assent rose in the crowd.

"You will all know soon enough," my father said, "but I say that man who sent the gold coin cannot be Richard Lander."

The messenger reached, again, inside his oilskins. "The man in the Sun Tavern knew he would need proof," he said, "and so he gave me this. For Miss Hannah Chelmsford."

He took out a small package, also wrapped in oilskin. I heard people drawing in their breaths, felt them watching me.

With shaking fingers, I undid the rawhide tie. Inside the oilskin was the most beautiful piece of silk fabric I had ever seen. It was delicately brocaded in gold thread.

There were ohs and ahs from the assembled.

With the fabric was a hand-scrawled note, from Richard.

"Read it," everyone begged.

I read it. " *'For your quilt, dear Hannah. I hope this is a little better offering than that square of muslin from my shirt. With love, Richard.'* "

Tears streamed down my face. I held up the fabric for all to see. "It's from Richard," I said. "And this is his writing. He's back, he's returned to us."

"Let me see, Hannah." Cabot had come to stand beside me. I gave him the square of silk. He looked at the note. "It's Richard's writing," he said. "I delivered many a note for him. I know."

Father took the square of silk from me, fingered it, puzzled. He looked unbelieving.

Mr. Hiller set down his goblet of wine. "Good people," he said, "as much as I hate to leave your pleasant company on this ungodly day, I am off at once to Winter Island to perform the duties for which I am paid. Are there any investors here who would like to accompany me?"

Three men asked for their coats.

"Let me go, Hannah," Cabot begged. "Let me, please. I want to see Richard. I want to board the *Prince*."

I hugged him close and looked at Father. He scowled.

"Please, Hannah?" Cabot was begging.

He came up to my shoulder now, in height. He would soon be a man. And I minded how he'd never been allowed to go anywhere, how he'd been denied his chance to go west with Father. How Father had always thwarted him when he wanted to do something.

"How will you get back home this night?" I asked him.

"I'll stay with Richard. Wherever he stays. He'll let me, Hannah. I'll be the welcoming committee. Please?"

I knew I should say no. But I could not deny the look in my brother's eyes. "All right," I said. "But dress warmly and be careful."

He was near beside himself with joy. As he ran for his oilskins and the men waited for him I met my father's eyes. He glared at me. I glared back in defiance.

After the small party departed, Reverend Bentley offered a prayer of thanksgiving for Richard's return. Not to be outdone, Father proposed a toast then for Richard Lander and the *Black Prince*.

Richard home! My head was swimming. I could scarcely believe it.

Chapter Twenty-four

The next morning the storm was gone. I awoke not only to sun and blue skies, but to the ringing of church bells. On a Monday? I sat up in bed. What disaster had befallen us now?

Mattie came into the room, smiling and bearing my tray of hot chocolate.

"Has a vessel been broken to pieces offshore?" I asked. "Is a rescue operation underway?" I felt dazed, confused.

She set down the tray. "Good morning," she said cheerfully. "The baby is fed and bathed. You must decide what to wear down to breakfast. How about this?" And she'd taken out both my green silk and my best blue printed cotton.

"Are you mad, Mattie? Why should I dress so for breakfast? And why are the bells ringing? You didn't answer."

"You might want to dress for breakfast because you have a visitor," she said. And the way she said it made my heart leap inside me.

I looked at her, disbelieving. "He's here?"

She nodded happily. "In person. No ghost. He's in the dining room this very minute. Talking with your father."

"My father?"

"You're starting to sound like the village idiot, Hannah. He's brought Cabot home. They're waiting for you, for breakfast. Oh Hannah, my brother is home! And I'm so proud of him!"

"You should be. Oh, I'm shaking. Oh, Mattie, help me dress, please."

As she helped me with the hooks and eyes on my dress she told me how people were rushing to the wharf to see the *Prince*. "Richard said she will be dropping anchor in Salem Harbor by noon. I'm so happy for you, Hannah," she said. "I know how you sore missed him. We all have."

I turned to face her. "Dear Mattie." I looked into the unblinking blue eyes. "I know how you miss Lawrence. I've begged him, for seven months now in my letters, to come home."

She nodded. "He won't be home until they find Thankful. In every letter he writes he says he feels guilty because Thankful is gone. But it's more than that; it's become an obsession with him. In his last letter he said he's joining with some expedition against the Shawnees who have been attacking along the Ohio River."

"I shall write to him, Mattie. And tell him tomorrow to come home. If I can do nothing else for him, I can do that. There's no need for him to fight the Indians."

She hugged me. "I love you dearly," she said, "but Lawrence feels the need. And I'm afraid we must let him do it, Hannah, if we want him back ever again."

"Richard?"

He stood up as I came into the sun-filled dining room.

I had not seen him or heard from him in thirteen months. There had been days when I could not conjure up his face. But not a day had gone by when he was not in front of my mind.

I perceived instantly that he was changed. Those who had said they thought they saw his ghost in town yesterday were not far from wrong. He was thinner, almost gaunt. His face was sun-browned, his hair long and tied in a queue behind his neck, military fashion. But it was the eyes that struck me. They were deeper set. There were hollows under them.

I knew, at once, looking into those eyes, that he had gone places that were further away than geography could explain. And I knew they were places that no civilized man had gone before.

"Hannah," his voice, warm and strong, found the aching places inside me even before he could cross the carpet and take me in his arms, right in front of my father and brother.

"We must talk now, Hannah."
"Yes."

"There are things you should know."

We were walking in my garden. Supper of that same day was over. And this was our first chance to be alone.

All afternoon we'd been at the wharf. Salutes from other vessels had been fired in the *Black Prince's* honor as she sailed into Salem Harbor, where dock workers guided her into her berth. A crowd had come to watch and to marvel at Richard's cargo.

Pepper. That was the bulk of his cargo, 158,544 pounds of it.

Richard had brought the first shipment of black pepper to America from Sumatra.

He had also brought 28 pounds of Hyson tea, nankeen, porcelain, and silk. And many curios. Guarded by his men, the curios were on display at the wharf: various specimens of shells, the tooth of an elephant, a petrified mushroom cap and stem, two specimens of boxes in gold, intricately designed with openwork and flowers, done by the Malays.

He had not told me yet of his adventures. He'd come to supper wearing the whitest of shirts, ruffled, with a black silk stock. His trousers were made of nankeen. He looked like the successful merchant.

"I'm so proud of you, Richard!" I said.

He stopped walking and looked down at me earnestly. "Are you?"

"Yes."

"You don't know everything."

"You will tell me in time."

"No, I must tell you now. I've killed someone, Hannah."

I waited.

"You are not surprised?"

"Richard, I know you have been to ungodly places. On the *Prince* today I saw your charts in your cabin. I know you went around the Gold Coast and the Cape of Good Hope. Then where?"

"To Bombay, then Sumatra."

"I know you must have had to do things to survive."

He nodded and sighed. "On the coast of Sumatra we were attacked by a French privateer. Its captain thought we were an English vessel. They boarded the *Prince* and we thought they were Malays, who often attack. It was dark. Before the mistake was discovered, one Frenchman's hand was cut off. And I killed a French lieutenant."

"They attacked you, Richard."

"Yes. But I wanted you to know."

"You are a hero," I said. "For your courage and your seaman's skill, for discovering a new trade route, and for bringing the first cargo of pepper to America."

We stood in silence for a moment. I sensed that something more was troubling him.

"I thought I would never see you again," I said. "And I needed you so, Richard. Especially when I heard about Thankful."

"A terrible thing, Hannah. I hate myself that I wasn't here for you."

"But you were! I felt your presence! I heard you telling me to have faith that she was alive!"

He smiled ruefully.

"And when I had to decide about the baby! Oh, Richard, I didn't know what to do! Did I do right, saying I would keep her? Do you mind?"

He squeezed my hand. "No, Hannah. Why should I mind?"

"Father said you would."

He grunted. "I'm not your father, Hannah."

"He's so evil, Richard. I can't wait to marry, so I can get Cabot and Georgianna out of his house and away from his influence. He's made Lawrence feel so guilty about Thankful that poor Lawrence may spend years on the frontier looking for her if I don't do something about it. He told Louis the only way he would allow me to keep the baby is if Louis searched for Thankful until she was found. And you see how he uses little Georgianna to enhance his reputation!

"What's wrong, Richard? Something *is* wrong. Tell me."

"Dear Hannah," he said. "I must go back."

"Back?" I looked at him stupidly.

"Yes. The trade route is still a secret. But I don't think it will stay that way long. I must make another voyage, while the market is still mine. There were import duties of over nine thousand dollars. There is one investor I must pay off immediately.

That doesn't leave me with much, after I pay the crew, outfit the *Prince* for her next voyage, and invest in enough ginseng, silver, tobacco, and spices along my way, to sell or trade."

What was he saying?

And then I knew. Out of everything he'd just said, one phrase stuck fast in my mind. "What investor must you pay off immediately?" I asked.

He didn't answer.

"My father? It's my father, isn't it? Is he badgering you for a return on his money?"

He shook his head and sighed again. "Yes, it's your father," he admitted. "But he isn't badgering me for anything. I just want to pay him off. I never want to be beholden to your father again. For anything."

"Then why did you accept his money, Richard? There must have been several speculators willing to take the risk. Mr. Prince, Mr. Hodge, Mr. Silsbee, Mr. Crowninshield. All the codfish aristocrats are speculators."

"I didn't accept his money, Hannah. I never would have, had I known it was his money. He invested it through others. I just found out when I met with my investors aboard the *Prince* this afternoon. He bought shares through Mr. Crowninshield, Mr. Pierce, and Mr. Nichols."

I felt the anger flow through my veins. "I told you he was evil," I said. "How many shares does he own in this venture, Richard?"

"Almost half," he said.

"My God!"

"Yes, Hannah, and that's why I must go back. My next voyage will be more profitable. And I want to pay him back before we marry."

Only then did I understand what he was saying. I felt myself sway. I had to grip his forearms with my hands. "Are you saying we can't marry until you return from your next voyage?"

"Do you want him to own us, Hannah?"

"He can never own me, Richard. And no one can ever own you."

"He owns near half of what I have now. I don't want that, Hannah. I and my family have been in his grip as long as I can remember. I don't want to start my marriage that way. I want to be free of him."

I felt the anguish in him, heard the pleading note in his voice. Could I demand that he marry me now? I had every right to. And I knew that if I did, Richard would comply with my wishes.

But he was right. We would be owned by my father. He would hold his iron hand over us. I had no doubt in my mind that he had invested in Richard's venture simply so he could continue to control us.

No, I could not do that to Richard, much as I wanted to marry him, long as I had waited. I could not do that to him any more than Mattie could force Lawrence to come home. Richard had worked and fought all his life to become his own man, to fish on his own hook, as Yankee fishermen said years earlier. And I knew that if I kept him under my father's hand, even until he completed his next voyage, that he could not do this. It would demean him.

And perhaps ruin our marriage. No, I vowed silently, I will not do that. I will not have my marriage tainted, as my mother's was.

"The voyage is dangerous, isn't it, Richard? There are pirates, hurricanes, privateers."

"I can outwit them all." He smiled sadly.

In the gathering twilight I looked up into his dear face.

"Will you wait for me, Hannah," he asked, "and marry me when I return?"

"This is the fourth time you have asked me to marry you, Richard Lander," I said. I was crying.

He took me in his arms and held me for dear life. "One of these times I'm going to be able to do it," he said.

I felt the thinness of him as he held me. I thought of all he'd been through, all I'd been through. And I knew we were irrevocably bound, we two. That we had been bound, since I was four and he was ten. And that nothing and no one, not pirates, hurricanes, privateers, or my father, could keep us apart.

Epilogue

Thankful
November 1791

The girl awoke in her wigewa before there was any movement from the others. It was her job to be the first up to fetch wood for the morning's dying fire. She'd always hated the chore. But it was one of the few she had, so she could not complain.

She took a moment to snuggle under her buffalo robe before stirring. Beside her the dog moved, thumped his tail, and nuzzled her hand. She patted him. He was one of the things she knew she should be grateful for. That she was allowed her own dog. And that she had people to love and protect her. They slept now on the other side of the wigewa, Old Mother and her son, Cat-That-Prowls. He was an important warrior of the Kispokoth sept of the Shawnee tribe.

They called her Much Favored. For that is the way they regarded her in the tribe. From the beginning she had been treated well, not beaten, like most prisoners. She'd been given more than enough to eat, presented with fine beaded dresses and moccasins and a warm furry robe in winter. They had even allowed her to keep her own horse.

She was favored because of her eyes.

When she was first brought into camp they had gathered around her and stared at her. One blue eye and one green one. Never had they seen such eyes. Much excitement had generated around her. Blue Jacket, the chief, a white man who had voluntarily joined the Shawnees in 1771 when he was seventeen, made a speech. It was a sign that she had come to them, he said. It meant good fortune, and she would be well treated. He gave her to Old Mother and Cat-That-Prowls. Old Mother taught her the Shawnee ways.

Thankful learned quickly. At first she missed her father and cried for him at night and waited for him or her brother to come for her.

But they had not come.

So she stopped waiting. And looked around her. And she started to realize something. These people kept their word. They revered her, spoiled her. The other children in camp deferred to her, looked up to her. The women were intrigued when she showed them her piece of the quilt, which she had had in her saddlebags when captured. They crowded around when she worked on it. They brought forth pieces of doeskin and pelts to add to it. And asked to learn how to work on it, too.

She had taught them. It added to her stature. Everything she did was a source of wonderment to them.

Once she realized what power she had, Thankful Chelmsford decided to make the best of her situation. She'd been thirteen when she was taken. She was now sixteen, a lovely young woman. Life was turning into a fine adventure.

And then there was the very fact of Cat-That-Prowls.

Never had she met any man, Indian or white, who was so handsome and tall and proud. At first he had taken her under his wing, as a little sister, teaching her to fish, showing her how to identify certain wild roots, how to track animals, taking her on long rides and showing her the land. It was Cat-That-Prowls who taught her to appreciate the land, and told her the secrets of nature. He was far better an older brother than that prig Lawrence had ever been, she decided.

As she matured, however, he started to tease her and regard her in a different way. A way that made her blush and tingle.

Within the last year she had decided she was in love with Cat-That-Prowls, and he with her. The elders in the village, which was situated in northern Ohio, nudged each other and gave sly winks when they saw them together. Old Mother watched over them carefully, giving approving glances.

Cat-That-Prowls gave Thankful many little gifts. Often those gifts were books that were taken when whites were captured. And when she read from those leaves that talked, as the Shawnees called the books, they were more sure than ever that she possessed good magic.

So life was good for Thankful. As the seasons turned, one into the other, as she allowed herself to be pulled into the rhythm of the Shawnee life, she began to realize that life could be good. She learned about family love for the first time.

To these people family meant much. She compared them to her own family and realized how little her people had known of real love. She had a mother now, to care for her, to caress her when she was fretful, to teach her how to be a woman. As time went by she stopped thinking of her own family. They had never been happy anyway. They did not know what happiness meant.

She had pushed them to the back of her mind. Until yesterday.

Yesterday they had brought the white prisoner into camp. Thankful had seen him. He was now in the marque that was part of the booty captured from the army of General St. Clair in a recent battle.

The Shawnees had been victorious that autumn in defeating the armies of both Generals Harmar and St. Clair. And they had not taken many prisoners. Most of their captives had been killed. So this man must be special.

Yesterday Thankful had thought she recognized him, though he was beaten and dirty. Those eyes. She had seen them someplace before.

And then, last evening when she fell asleep, her own eyes hypnotized by the fire, she knew who the prisoner was.

He was Hannah's old beau, Louis. Thankful had been a child when she had met him in Philadelphia, years ago. But she never forgot a face.

She knew, immediately, what she must do, of course. And that was why for once she was grateful that her job was to be up early and fetch wood.

She got up from her bed of covered soft boughs, put on her moccasins, drew a light blanket around her, and went outside. It was so cold. A light snow was falling. In her hand she had a knife, given to her by Cat-That-Prowls. She walked through the sleeping camp, past wigewas that loomed out of the morning mist, past horses and sleeping dogs, to the end of the camp where stood the marque.

She slipped inside.

Here, too, the fire was low. The prisoner was awake, however, and stared at her through cat's eyes, knowing and slate-blue. She said nothing, but knelt down beside him. He was tied at both wrists. His feet were bound, also.

He watched her movements as she cut the ropes that bound his ankles, then his wrists. He sat up and rubbed his wrists.

"Why do you do this?" he asked.

"You must escape," she whispered. "Quickly now. Go from this place, before the camp comes to life."

She had turned to leave, but he stood up and put a strong hand on her wrist. "You're Thankful, aren't you?" he said.

She looked down at the strong browned hand on her wrist and said nothing for a moment. Then, "I am Much Favored," she said.

"Yes, and I'm President Washington. Look, I'd know those eyes and that hair anywhere. Met you once when you were a young 'un. Been hunting you for three long years. You know who I am?"

"Louis," she said. "Hannah's beau. Go now. Back to the East. Or they will kill you."

"They won't kill me," he said. "I'm a friend of Blue Jacket's. I'm an Indian agent, well respected."

"No white man is a friend of Blue Jacket's these days. He seeks to avenge the capture of the fifty-eight women and children taken in raids on Kickapoo, Potawatomi, and Miami towns, in September."

"They weren't killed. They were marched to Cincinnati."

"They were *taken*," she spat out. "While the men were away. If you know what is good for you, you will leave now. Or they may torture you before they kill you."

"Right. Let's be on our way. Can you get my horse?"

"I am staying here."

He stopped, mid-movement, and blew on his cold hands to warm them. The slate-blue eyes surveyed her knowingly. "They made a Shawnee of you, hey?"

"They treat me well. I am special here."

"You're special at home, too. Why in God's name would you stay? I've spent three years hunting you! Your father is near daft by now. Your brother Lawrence is wandering up and down the whole territory seeking you, half crazed with grief. When he isn't fighting Indians."

She smiled serenely. "My father does not know what love is. He kept Hannah from you when she was fifteen, did he not?"

Louis nodded. The slate-blue eyes went sad.

"I should go back to a father like this? No one can keep me from Cat-That-Prowls. As for Lawrence, tell him the girl he seeks is no more. And it is just as well. Tell him to go home and do his painting."

"Listen, girl. You're white. You belong with your people."

"These are my people now," she said. "They treat me well. I am favored. Because of my eyes. They are convinced I bring good fortune to them. Have they not won many important victories over the blue coat soldiers since I came?"

"Important, yes. They cut Colonel John Hardin's Kentucky militia to pieces, fall of '90. To say nothing of what they did to the rest of General Harmar's forces. This fall they wiped out Harmar and St. Clair. And now they're attacking Kentucky settlements. Favored because of your eyes, hey?"

She minded the way his own eyes went over her, as a man's eyes go over a woman.

"I saw you yesterday when they brought me in," he said, "saw you with that young warrior. It's more than your eyes, missy. Look here, have they harmed you?"

"No one has harmed me. And no one has made of me anything I do not want to be. Can't you understand that?"

"Yes, I can," he said softly. "I understand more than you think I do, missy. I had an Indian wife."

She stared at him, unbelieving. "You?"

"Yes."

"What happened to her?"

"She was killed a while back. In an attack on her village by Kentuckians. I know the Shawnees. I visited their camps and was made welcome many times when my wife lived. I know how they hold the family in high esteem. I have a baby who is half-Indian."

She gasped. "Where is this child?"

"Back East. Your sister Hannah is minding her for me."

"Hannah?" Some of the old mischief came back into Thankful's face and it was her first impulse to say something saucy about Hannah. Then the look was replaced by one of sadness. "Hannah will mind her well for you," she said. "Are you and Hannah to marry then?"

"No." He sighed and shook his head. "She was to marry Richard Lander. But they haven't yet, I hear. I don't know why."

Thankful nodded, understanding. "I think she always loved Richard, though she was too prissy to admit it."

"Your sister Hannah was never prissy," he said. "She has turned into a fine specimen of a woman. And I shall always love her."

How like Hannah, Thankful minded, with some of her old resentment, how like her to have two men love her at once. Then the resentment vanished. For a moment there was silence inside the marque. Thankful heard snow falling on its roof.

"You'd best be sure of what you're about, missy," Louis advised. "Make darn sure. There is no going back after you stay with the Indians a while. I've been present at many prisoner exchanges. I've seen whites sent across the river, after years of living like you're living, crying and refusing to go back to their white families. It isn't something you ever want to see. Or be part of."

Thankful nodded.

"There's no going back after a while," Louis said sadly.

Thankful nodded. "There is no going back for me now. And I am sure. It is getting light. You must go."

He picked up his hat, put it on. She retrieved his musket and knife and hatchet from a corner and handed them to him.

"Why did you cut me loose?" Louis asked.

"So you can go back and tell them you saw me. And that I choose not to come home. And that I am happy and have a good man and am much favored."

"Favored." Louis sighed and shook his head. "Don't know as I can ever tell your father I found you and you refused to come back with me, missy."

"Why?"

Louis shook his head in dismay. "Can't. You wouldn't understand. You don't know your father for what he really is. We have an agreement, he and I. He's letting Hannah keep my child, long as I search for you. If I go back and tell him the truth, he could get so angry, he could refuse my child a home."

Thankful smiled. It was a serene smile, an accepting smile.

"You don't believe that about your father, do you?" Louis asked.

"Yes, I believe it," Thankful said. "There was a time I would not. But I do now. Why do you think I have chosen to stay here? Will you tell Hannah?"

Louis looked surprised at this display of maturity and understanding from one whom he had known to be so spoiled, so thoughtless. "If you want me to, yes, I will," he said softly. "But then I'll have to pretend I'm still searching for you. So my own little girl can have a good home."

He let his eyes go over her again, not in the

way a man's eyes go over a woman now, but with a newfound appreciation and sense of wonder.

As he turned to unloosen the flap of the marque, Thankful put a hand on his arm. "In return for your understanding," she said, "may I tell you some things I have heard?"

Louis's eyes narrowed. "Yes."

"I have heard Tecumseh and Blue Jacket and others talking. Yes, there have been great victories, they say. And they will fight to the death. But it will only be a matter of time until the people from the Thirteen Fires overrun them. They know this. They are not stupid."

He looked at her in disbelief. "And you choose to stay?"

"I have found love here. For the first time in my life. If these are the last years for these people, I want to be part of them, yes. And thank God He has allowed me to be."

"And when they are overrun? What of your children?"

"I will worry that matter when the time comes."

Louis shook his head again and went through the tent flap. She directed him toward the horses. Snow was falling harder now, a fine, thin sheet of it. He slipped up onto one of the horses, bareback. She took off her blanket and gave it to him.

"Will you tell Hannah something for me?" she asked.

He nodded.

"Tell her I am working on my piece of the quilt.

Tell her it is fashioned out of pieces of doeskin and some beaded fabric. She would not recognize it now, but tell her, just the same."

Louis nodded, looked at her for one last time, and rode off.

She stood in the cold, watching him ride away.

If Louis had turned, he would have seen tears coming down the face of Much Favored. But he did not turn. He had learned by now that life was less painful if you never looked back.

Author's Note

The idea for this book was born out of my desire to write about a family that gets torn apart, seemingly by events outside the home, but actually due to dark undercurrents from within, undercurrents that reach out from the past, like threads which begin to unravel under the pressure of everyday life and threaten the very fabric of its existence.

I also wanted an object as the centerpiece, an object that is handed down and survives the years when the family unity is all but gone. How many times have I wondered what wonderful tales an object could tell over the generations. A yellowed and dog-eared original copy of the Declaration of Independence, for instance, which recent news stories tell us was found at a flea market hidden in a picture frame. How many hands did it pass through in a little over two hundred years? Such ideas have always intrigued me.

I decided to make my "object" a quilt. I have always had a spiritual kinship with quilts. I once purchased one on vacation in Vermont, in a far flung hamlet on a rainy day. It is of the log cabin design and, in attempting to put it back into condition, I found that the patches were previously repaired by diligent hands. The swatches of fabric used looked as if the previous restoration attempts were done during the Depression. Who originally made it? Who restored it? The idea haunts me.

Another reason for deciding on a quilt was because I wanted something that could be divided amongst the three sisters, Hannah, Abby, and Thankful, when they become separated, with the surviving pieces identifying their descendants.

This, of course, would necessitate making my book into a series. But why not? Young people love a series. But—an historical series? Again why not? Many letters from young readers beg me to write sequels so they can pick up on the characters in my books whom they have learned to love.

Next I had to determine the geographic location for my family. They must have something to do with fabrics. The natural conclusion was that the Chelmsfords would have their beginnings firmly rooted in an experiment in cotton manufacturing that eventually blooms into the Lowell mills in Massachusetts.

In reading of the origins of the Lowell mills I learned that one of the first attempts at manufacturing cotton in America was in Beverly, Massachusetts, near Salem.

I would place my family in Salem! I had fallen in love with the town researching *A Break With*

Charity, my novel on the Salem witch trials. Of course, I had no idea what Revolutionary War and post-Revolutionary War Salem were like until I read *The World Turned Upside Down* by Ronald N. Tagney.

In Tagney's book and in *Salem, Maritime Salem in the Age of Sail*, published by the U.S. Department of the Interior, and such formidable reading as *Salem Vessels and Their Voyages*, by George Granville Putnam, I discovered Salem's value as a port before, during and after the war.

I learned about ships, trade routes, privateers, counting houses, the lives of sea captains and the merchants who backed them financially. I learned of the elegance of the Salem homes occupied by colorful and daring merchants determined to forge new trade routes and make Salem the leading port in the country, following the Revolution.

I learned the role Salem played in the American Revolution.

Out of this grew my plot.

To most people, reading such "dry" matter as the above-mentioned, is an overwhelming task. But just perusing a page of Putnam's book that lists the arrivals and departures of Salem vessels, activated my fantasies.

Imagine how delighted I was to discover, in Barbara Tuchman's *The First Salute*, another wonderful book, the explanation of how long it took a vessel of those times to make the journey from North America to Europe and back, to learn that the eastward passage was called "downhill" and took three weeks to a month, as opposed to "uphill," the voyage back to America which took three months.

I am indebted to Tuchman's research for such information as well as for the instructions I needed to "turn the *Black Prince*," and the makeup of the islands of the West Indies, essential information for my voyage of Abby and Nate in the *Swamp Fox*.

I had already decided that I wanted one sister to be taken by Indians. So I was equally thrilled, reading Tagney's book, to discover that on December 3, 1787 (exactly when I wanted my book to begin) an advance party departed from Salem to settle in Ohio Territory, following the opening of the Northwest Territory to settlers after the war.

Indeed, it was the Reverend Manessah Cutler of Ipswich, Massachusetts, who was one of the chief promoters of the Ohio Company. I used the timetable of this Salem expeditionary force as a guide for the settlers in my book.

In all my historical novels I attempt, in the author's note, to separate what is real from what I made up for the sake of the story.

All my characters, with the exception of Reverend William Bentley, D.D., are fictionalized. However, Nathaniel Chelmsford is a composite. Part of him is based on Church Boott who came from Derbyshire, England, to Boston in 1783 and is described in *Kirk Boott, Master Spirit of Early*

Lowell, by Brad Parker, as "the midwife of the first major textile center in the United States."

Part of Nathaniel Chelmsford is Boott's son, Kirk, whom Parker describes as a "lordly, imperious, and unpopular figure." Referring to a book, *Golden Threads*, by Hannah Josephson, Parker tells us that Josephson described Kirk Boott as a "willful, arrogant, and imperious martinet who exhibited haughty airs to his social inferiors."

I also likened Nathaniel Chelmsford to Francis Cabot Lowell, who was one of the founders of the Lowell mills.

The three sisters, Hannah, Abigail, and Thankful, are of my own making, as are their brothers Lawrence and Cabot. Louis Gaudineer, Hannah's star-crossed Pennsylvania militiaman, is fictitious also, although there were many like him who went west to try to keep peace between the settlers and the Indians.

There was no Richard Lander in history, but his father did exist. Tagney tells us of Peter Lander, commander of the ninety-ton schooner, *Sturdy Begger*. In 1775 a legislative committee visited Salem to investigate allegations that Elias Hasket Derby had imported coffee and other goods from Dominica, going against the First Continental Congress's regulations decreeing cessation of trade with Great Britain and her possessions.

Derby was cleared of all charges, as often happens today when someone is a financial success and a well-known figure. However, his captain,

Peter Lander, took the blame. Lander's suicide is my own invention, as is his son, Richard, who tries to make up for what was done to his father by becoming a leading Salem merchant in his own right.

As for Richard Lander's "secret" voyage to Sumatra in pursuit of the pepper trade route, that is based on the account in *Salem Vessels and Their Voyages* of the voyage of the *Rajah* in 1795, commanded by Captain Jonathan Carnes, who is cited as being the first one to open such a trade route and bring black pepper to the United States.

However, there are two different dates given in the record books for Captain Carnes's visit to the northwest coast of Sumatra. In Joseph B. Felt's *Annals of Salem*, the date pepper was first brought to America by Carnes is 1789. That first voyage to Sumatra by Carnes, whatever the year, was shrouded in mystery so he could keep the trade route a secret. I needed just such a sense of mystery for Richard's voyage, both to build tension in the plot and to have him be suspected of dealing in the slave trade by Salem's very anti-slavery population.

Richard's return, in a terrible storm, is based on the story of the return of Nathaniel Bowditch in the *Putnam* from Sumatra to Salem in December 1803, as recounted by Paul Rink in his article *Nathaniel Bowditch, The Practical Navigator*, in *American Heritage*, August 1960.

Nate Videau is a character of my own invention,

as I needed a Southern ship's master to elope with Abigail. I have always been intrigued by the story of Francis Marion, the Swamp Fox of the Revolution. Marion married a woman who gave him and his band of guerillas aid in the war. Not much is known about Mary (or Esther) Videau, except that she married Marion when the war ended. Her brother Nate is pure fiction.

There was a Captain William Burnaby. In late May, 1775, he was the master of the *HMS Merlin*, one of the British warships that patrolled offshore Marblehead and Salem. Captain Burnaby is reported to have "come ashore and purchased bread in Salem." Trade with the enemy was frowned upon by the inhabitants of Salem, of course. The rest—how he became Cabot's father, is of my own making.

Reverend Bentley's character is taken from volume one of *The Diary of William Bentley, D.D.* edited by Peter Smith. I have tried to depict him faithfully and accurately as one of Salem's most notable and compassionate pastors.

That the *Black Prince* is a privateer in my book is a matter of history. There were scores of privateers operating along the coastal seaboard of New England during the Revolution. Twelve or thirteen were Salem-based.

In actuality the *Black Prince* was a two hundred twenty-ton privateer carrying eighteen guns with a crew of one hundred thirty, owned by Nathaniel West of Beverly/Salem. The ship was part of the expeditionary force of eighteen state vessels and privateers whose captains attempted to take back from the British their foothold in New England when the enemy "is got into the river of Penobscot."

What followed was the ill-fated Penobscot Expedition, a disaster for the Americans, a terrible blow to the pride and resources of Massachusetts. It accounted for private losses which exceeded one million pounds.

Historically, the *Black Prince* was burned and ruined. In my book, too, she is charred and ruined in that venture, a symbol of the losses to Massachusetts's brave merchants and seamen in the war. And a symbol of the charred pride of the Landers family, restored by Richard Lander, as the ship itself is restored by him to her former glory.

The house the Chelmsford family occupies still exists in Salem. It is now a National Park office site. Known as the Hawkes House, it was actually built by Elias Hasket Derby in 1780 and purchased by Benjamin Hawkes, the owner of a shipyard next to Derby Wharf, in 1800. It is a yellow clapboard Georgian mansion, once used by Derby to house prize goods taken by his Revolutionary privateers. It most suited my needs. However, there is no record of how it was furnished in the time period. So I had to call on my imagination and descriptions of other houses of the time for such details.

Having chronicled here some of the fragments of history I called into play to write my book, I can only hope to advise my readers of what is real and what I made up. The missing ingredient, of course, is the writer's imagination, the ability to pursue a dry book of facts for hours to finally seize some incidental piece of history that sets the mind aflame. This is how historical novelists work. We take data uninteresting to the lay person and fill in the dots between the facts with colorful characters and their motivation.

"We cannot escape history," Abraham Lincoln once said. As an historical novelist I do not want to. I wish to pursue it, to follow its winding paths in all my novels, and certainly intend to do just that in the two books that will complete this series, which will bring the family up to the era right before the Civil War and finally reunite them, with the pieces of the quilt sewn by their ancestors.

Ann Rinaldi
June 29, 1993

Bibliography

Eckert, Allan W. *Gateway to Empire*, New York: Bantam Books, 1984.

Graebner, William, and Leonard Richards, eds. *The American Record, Volume 1, Images of the Nation's Past*, New York: Alfred A. Knopf, 1982.

Graham, Gerald S. *The Royal Navy in the War of Independence*. London: Her Majesty's National Maritime Museum Stationery Office, 1976.

Nylander, Jane C. *Our Own Snug Fireside: Images of the New England Home, 1760–1860*. New York: Alfred A. Knopf, 1993.

Parker, Brad. *Kirk Boott, Master Spirit of Early Lowell*. Lowell: Landmark Printing Co., 1985.

Preston, Antony, David Lyon and John H. Batchelor. *Navies of the American Revolution*. Englewood Cliffs, N.J.: Prentice-Hall Inc., 1975.

Prucha, Francis Paul, *The Sword of the Republic, The United States Army on the Frontier, 1783–1846*, Lincoln: University of Nebraska Press, 1986.

Putnam, George Granville. *Salem Vessels and Their Voyages. A History of the Pepper Trade with the Island of Sumatra*. Salem: The Essex Institute, 1924.

Rink, Paul E. "Nathaniel Bowditch, The Practical Navigator," *American Heritage*, Volume XI, Number 5, August 1960.

Salem, Maritime Salem in the Age of Sail. Washington, D.C., National Park Service, Division of Publications for Salem Maritime National Historic Site, U.S. Department of the Interior, 1987 (in cooperation with the Peabody Museum and the Essex Institute, Salem, Massachusetts.)

Smith, Peter, *The Diary of William Bentley, D.D., Pastor of the East Church, Salem, Massachusetts*. Volume 1, April 1784–Dec. 1792, Gloucester, Massachusetts, Peter Smith, 1962.

Smith, Philip Chadwick Foster. *Captain Samuel Tucker (1747–1833) Continental Navy*. Salem: Essex Institute, 1976.

Tagney, Ronald N. *The World Turned Upside Down, Essex County During America's Turbulent Years, 1763–1790*. West Newbury: Essex County History, 1989.

Thom, James Alexander. *Panther in the Sky*. New York: Ballantine Books, 1989.

Tuchman, Barbara W. *The First Salute*. New York: Alfred A. Knopf, 1988.

About the Author

Ann Rinaldi is one of today's best-known writers of historical fiction for young adults. *Wolf by the Ears,* her first novel for Scholastic Hardcover, as well as three of her previous works, were named ALA Best Books for Young Adults. Ms. Rinaldi is also the recipient of an award from the DAR for her historical fiction.

Ann Rinaldi lives in Somerville, New Jersey, with her husband.